OSIRUS PART ONE

BODH SONAVANE

Contents

ASSASSIN'S MANSION
HIMACHAL PRADESH
PUNJAB
HARYANA
DEMOLISHED BUILDING
NEW DELHI
INDIA GATE

Acknowledgements

I want to thank my loving parents, brothers, cousins, Uncles & Aunts for supporting me and letting me write this book. I would also like to thank my other relatives, neighbours, and friends who encouraged me to write this book & supported me in the ways they could. They motivated me to write this book.

I want to thank my brother Yash Sonawane for editing out the mistakes I couldn't find and helping this book come together.

I would especially thank my computer Sir James, who encouraged me to publish this Book and supported me throughout its writing and publishing process.

I would also like to give a special thanks to this book's Co-Author and Critic, Shamit More who helped me write this book and make decisions to make the book good as he's an Author himself (he even inspired me to write this book). He's the reason this book is good and exists.

I want to thank everyone who helped me write this book in any form, be it supporting, encouraging, etc. I am grateful that you all supported me in writing this book.

A humongous thanks to you guys :)

!trigger Warning!

• ix •

This book contains violence, strong language and mature themes which may not be suitable for some readers. Reader's discretion is advised.

Prologue

IT WAS such a night where you couldn't see anything. A large structure engulfed with violet flames. All of it was on a mountain. A heap of human corpses, and their blood bathed the grass beneath them. Between the small heap, Five people were standing holding their weapons, blood lust. The five of them desired to kill the man in front. The frontman, blood dried on his skin. rivers of blood, streams, were flowing from his head.

cocking up a broken spear.

All he is, injured but fearless...

CHAPTER ONE

It is 6 AM, and you can hear the loud noise from the flying Cars and bikes in the misty air. A huge celebration was planned at the **India Gate**. People were already there from 4 AM. Because after the clock strikes 7 AM, There would be peace no more, all that would be the crowd.

Meanwhile, A man with Blue eyes, His skin fair and rough. He had a Black shirt donned up, along with navy blue pyjamas. His name was Ernest. He was hastily brushing his teeth to reach there before 7:00 AM.

In his mind, "Goddamnit!" he said "should've kept an alarm at 5:30 AM."

He wondered why his toothpaste tasted like Antiseptic cream. Until he realized, it was indeed antiseptic cream.

"Ahh Damm-" he gagged and gargled the Cream out with water.

He was stressed about reaching on time. He quickly bathed, dried off, and donned a dark green sleeveless shirt, topped with a milk coffee brown jacket. Adding black cargo pants, shiny black boots, and tying his laces, he was ready.

Then Ernest ate bread with butter, mayonnaise and some curd on top.

He was consuming food like a literal vacuum cleaner. Then he drank water but the antiseptic cream's lingering was as powerful as the world's sourest candy, it didn't show any difference.

He then took his Hexagon-shaped key from a cupboard and closed it so hard that it made a loud noise of Around 65 decibels.

Ernest's Earbuds Shocked By the sudden noise he shouted "Ah, Crap!"

Then he Ran At extreme speed and took his black-covered phone, the food from the plastic basket he had stored, and the snacks packed in a black bag, filled up a whole 1-litre steel bottle of water. He finally closed the bright lights and turned on. Locking the door with The Hexagonal Key, he enrolled the car's door swiftly and perched inside, took one mint from the bag, and put it in his mouth. Then he started the car and drove it out of his home, he thought he would reach on time as there was plenty of time & so was driving at 100kmph. Ernest was there driving peacefully and checked the time it was 6:40 AM!

"Crap!" Muttered Ernest "I have to go faster than Ussain Bolt!"

Then He drove at 250KMph, struggling to even drive it, So much so that almost crashed it into a Liquid tree. Exceeding the speed limit simultaneously.

"(Frustrated) Holy cow!"

Ernest saw the time and it was 6:45 AM. Now the situation screwed up. He was driving in between cars, where he could go from, and after all that. Beside his window, peeped at the great colossal India Gate. In its good old Colour. With the name India appearing as Perfectly Carved. The road behind was covered in smoke. The grass in front of the gate, as much Earthy as it ever could be, the place was all calm and mysterious to look at.

"(gasps) Finally I've reached."

He had made It at 6:54 AM. Then his pocket began vibrating as he took out the phone. He got called by his friend named Shaun. Ernest picked it up.

"Where are you?"Asked Ernest.

"I am sitting on the grass for An Hour and a freaking half!"

"Wait? You came here one and a half hours ago, so why didn't you call me." Asked Ernest.

"Heck, I did call you but you didn't pick up The darn phone."

" Oh...hh yeah yeah it was on silent......." Said Ernest Embarrassed.

"Hey, there you are."

Then Shaun saw him distant, Ending the call. Shaun had brown eyes like an average Indian, a Red Jacket, a Black T-shirt, Cargo green sweatpants, donned with black boots, and his name sounded nasty asf.

He calls Ernest Out "Ernest! Come here at once."

Ernest went to meet Shaun. They stayed in the Grass. The terrain around sniffed Earthy, with the wind cold and blissful, and fortunate enough to be feeling it, 5 minutes left to get some peaceful time of ecstasy.

Shaun said, "It's Ecstasy, Not gonna lie. I feel great here, except for the fact that your mouth smells Antiseptic and mint cold. But something feels forgotten."

As he contemplated, he was struck by the fact that they had their one friend, yet to arrive.

"Ah, crap." Said, Shaun.

"The hell happened?" Asked Ernest.

"**Osirus**, that lazy-Ass dawg creature."

"What about him?" Asked Ernest "Oh, yeah that guy. He has not replied to any calls, I wonder what situation he's into"

"Now we'll wait, that's all we can wonder 'bout now."

They waited there for Osirus For 3 Hours......

They waited and waited, finally at 10 o'clock, 8 minutes. A man with pale ivory skin, dark brown and black eyes, with a decent amount of eyelashes, donning a black t-shirt, sheltered with a brown jacket on top, a sharp grey belt, amber blue jeans, and White Sneakers beautified with red patterns around them.

He came with lots of happiness and instantly found the two.

Ernest asked, "Why the hell are you so late **Osirus**?"

"Well I woke up at 6:30 AM," Said Osirus "And brushed but I accidentally brushed my teeth with..."

"Antiseptic cream right?" exclaimed Ernest "That's the thing I did."

"No bro, with Whipped cream, what you thought but I frickin don't know myself why I kept the whipped cream there." said Osirus "Instead of gargling it out, as it tasted good I swallowed it."

"Yuck, What the-" said Both Shaun And Ernest.

Osirus continued "I liked it then brushed my teeth, put up the hot shower and I slept, woke up at 8 'o'clock and already late!"

"Okay now this is getting repetitive and annoying, cut it." Said Ernest.

Shaun asked, "Why did you sleep ?"

Osirus said, "I then ate my breakfast which took 20 minutes to prepare." Continued "I then ate it and wore clothes and prepared to leave."

Shaun then again asked in a strict and loud tone " I asked why did you frickin sleep!!! "

Osirus replied swiftly "I did not sleep last night properly! As the electricity was gone I was feeling hot to such an extent that I was only able to sleep two hours, then I packed my bags but I accidentally forgot to take my phone and my door got locked and unfortunately, I forgot to take the keys, I tried to open the door with the things I got and it finally opened at 9:15 AM and I took the key along with my phone! I left the house and drove the car at 110 kilometres"

"Bro you don't have some backup or something man? You dumb piece of crap." Said Shaun"Plus driving at 110KMPH, knowing that the limit is more, still driving like if it's the 2020s."

Ernest then said, "Now the crowd is too much." and added, "You missed the peaceful point and still missed a lot of stuff."

"Now let it be, It's Diwali today let's celebrate !"

"Hell yeah!" said Ernest.

They had fun and explored the full place, ate there, enjoyed, danced, and finally decided to return to their homes.

It was 1 AM and a night where the moon's light could be reflected on mirrors and even on water. The street lights lit so bright that the three could see clearly that they were talking with each other.

"It was damn fun, right Shaun and Osirus?" Said Ernest in a tired tone.

"Yeah it was really fun, But I feel really (yawning) sleepy." Said Osirus in a really tired voice.

"Same here," said Shaun tired but having some bits of Energy left, so does Ernest.

As they were talking from the top of the building a force sharp wave fluid kind of thing swung at full speed on them. That thing had a Red bloody colour, White highlights, And a Red fluid thick as blood when mixed with Snake venom, it appeared in a red glow.

"what the hell was that." Said Osirus,

"Oh shoot!!" conveyed Ernest.

There on the top of the building were 4 Assassins, looking at them, the first on the right had fair pale skin, Eyes glowing red, and his hair covered under a jacket-like hood. Wearing a black tight sleek. Cocking up a dagger. A black mask. The second one, 6 feet tall, Holding up a Katana. The same uniform clothing with his mask having a design popping out. He had a fair white skin. The third one, had his hair pop out of his hood, His skin fair and smooth. The fourth one had a Better sleek. His mask foiled. He was olive-fair with a rough skin. He was all tight up with his fists.

The Third Assassin said, " You Scoundrels, Give us the Box You two and the Third pathetic Bastard, whoever he is".

" Shut up, you goons, we are not giving you that darn box" shouted Ernest.

"And if you try to be Notorious we are going to beat the crap out of ya," said Shaun.

" What the hell is going on guys, are they your relatives?" Asked Osirus in confusion.

" Don't worry Osirus, we will tell you everything first let us handle them" Said Ernest calmly.

Then the fourth Assassin said rudely "We are gonna knock you down hard now !".

Then Ernest Kicked up a small axe kept near a construction building and Shaun caught up a hammer, the Assassins came down the building and attacked them. Shaun attacked the third and fourth Assassin with his hammer and hit the Fourth Assassin's Jaw, the Jaw's breaking voice Kicked, and then He hit the Third Assassin on his Stomach and leg and he fell, then Shaun kicked his face. In that meantime, The fourth Assassin Healed his broken jaw a bit And then caught hold of The hammer.

Shaun said " Fudge! , he's got the hold, Ernest !!"

Meanwhile, Ernest stabbed the Axe in the Second Assassin's hind limb and then in the shoulder and sliced the first Assassin's Chin down, it started bleeding, he then kicked the first Assassin, As he heard the voice of Shaun.

"What?"

Shaun said, " Help out, This moron is on me."

Ernest went and held the fourth Assassin's throat and brought him back and was about to stab him then the first Assassin took the katana handle and hit it hard on Ernest's Head, Then Shaun took his hammer and threw the Fourth Assassin far and held the first Assassin back and started hitting him with the hammer, and the first one also fell.

Osirus, who was terrified to see such things, shouted in confusion " Shaun! , Ernest! What the hell are you guys doin'?"

The first Assassin Held Shaun's forelimbs with his legs and held his neck with his hands, then Shaun Went a bit down with his body trying to drop him but creating speed to throw him, and then he came back and threw him at the trash.

They Were fighting, then the fourth Assassin Went to Attack Osirus. He took a concrete rod and hit it on the Assassin's face. The rod broke into many pieces as if it were made of sand.

"Holy cow!!" shouted Osirus.

"Osirus !! Coming for you !!" they both said.

Then Shaun Took the Hammer and hooked the Fourth Assassin's neck's right side Spun him held him by his neck and threw him backside, Ernest had already caused havoc with the blood but unfortunately, all of the Assassins were alive, and still blood lusted to kill the trio and Shaun then yelled "Run!!"

They eventually began Running. Ernest and Shaun were running faster than a car, there were blue particles while they were running and the particles and energy were lustrous. They left Osirus behind by that speed and the Assassins were Chasing them.

Shaun slowed down a bit to say " Osirus !! Run frickin fast They will catch up and kick your butt".

The Assassins were catching up to the speed and the fourth Assassin had flowed his katana to slice Osirus's head off he even jumped to slit him in half and he slipped then he disappeared leaving Violet purple particles as if he teleported from there or ran extremely fast, but it wasn't Osirus in his consciousness, Osirus made it far though, really far away and Ernest And Shaun also reached after Distracting the Assassins, they were confused to see Osirus in such a speed. They went inside an under-construction building in which no one was there.

Shaun Shouted and asked, "How in the world did you run that fast !?"

Osirus conveyed screaming and shouting " I don't know !!! Why the hell does it happen !!!!, like! when my Abusive Uncle used to abuse me, I went unconscious and he is well... bleeding !! or when I was bullied like a dog in school and suddenly I black out and next all I can see is all the bullies are lying knocked up to their Ass." Then Osirus calmed and slowed down a bit and spoke but still in a high voice and spoke, "(gasps) It's so weird, and you idiots thought I have good fighting skills, but it's not like that maybe I have some kinda split personality disorder, maybe someone is controlling my body to protect me, But what's your deal with them?"

Ernest whispered in Shaun's ear "Is he who we think ?"

Shaun whispered in Ernest's ear "Same lemme ask, the name sounds kinda similar, shit we didn't consider it in all those years, how much of Stupids are we, man."

Shaun asked, " Wait, are you **Osirus,** Harsh's son?"

Osirus Stoke froze surprised, hearing the question after all these years. His eyes widened up,

In his mind " How the hell do they know my full damn name."

Then he snapped "How the hell do you know all of this shit, huh?" How do you guys use the magic- Oh you are the slave of that filthy old wizard, trying to manipulate me. My most important childhood was already screwed over by him."

His voice got higher.

"He took away my parents...."

His eyes began turning red. "-made me a good-for-nothing orphan."

"What else does he want from me? After already intoxicating my childhood?"

As the two heard it, Ernest lost it completely and snapped "Scorpious shitted your life up? Are you serious? He's the reason why you're not done for and "Intoxicating", let's not talk about your family, it's another bullcrap Emoish thing on its own. You are just blaming other people for your sufferings and no one gives a damn crap about it. I know you are just a prick who is sad but this is not the way moron."

Osirus was all stoked and froze upon hearing it. He couldn't say anything but only put his head down. His anger, the fire in him was short-lived.

"The hell do you want?" whispered Osirus.

"Absolutely heck nothing after hearing you." Said, Shaun.

Ernest snapped "Go, live your stupid coward-ish life."

The two turned behind to walk away, disappointed and agitated.

Osirus felt Guilty after hearing and with a heavy heart, yet the courage he said "Wait. I'll help you eliminate them.

"Come back?" Said Shaun "What did you just say??"

"I'll help you."

Shaun then burst out in laughter "Hah! The hell did he say Ernest you heard."

"Why are you laughing?"

"Because you can't do shit." Said Shaun "You are just a stupid, coward, freak and an Emo guy who thinks the whole world's Trauma is yours. You'll be wet in your pants helping us. You will be attacked, Almost killed and so much shit you will be crying about cause that's all you got."

Osirus replied, "I am ready for whatever the hell happens".

Finally, Ernest sighed "Fine, then come to stay at my home. Take your clothes & everything, we are going to the place where scorpious trained us, so he can train you, and also to secure ourselves from the Assassins and the box, these are B tier Assassins, they used to be S-tier Assassins that's why even your father had to sacrifice himself."

"So we are going where scorpious trained you guys," said Osirus "That's okay but what is there in the box? "

"The box basically contains the powers of the old leader who was damn strong, they want to become S-class Assassins as well as to become stronger and clear their agenda, which is to control the world how they want, and they probably might be having other agendas, but they work under a big organization who gives them ranking." Explained Ernest.

"That's the basic context, even we are not purely aware," Muttered Shaun " As we don't even know how they came into existence only the other Assassin groups know about it."

"Fine, I will help you guys out, and then might probably think about joining I will first think, I am not yet sure if should I become like you I will think of that". Osirus said, "Now lemme go and bring my clothes in a bag and the things required, like weapons and stuff, even though I don't have any weapons, I will search for something that can damage those idiots."

Osirus then goes home with the car packs his bags takes food and everything he requires and then goes with the bags to Ernest's home. They slept there.

CHAPTER TWO

It was 5 AM when Osirus was sleeping and then Ernest woke him up by Putting an annoying phone Alarm. It made Osirus feel the loud noise and annoyance sensation, he felt it in his nerves and it made the hair on his body stand he opened his eyes wide open with red nerves appearing and then he woke up and said in annoyance,

"Ernest !!! Why !!! It's so hell annoying man least play a good alarm man !!"

Ernest said, " Forgot we have to go to Kashmir." Osirus questioned" Wait? Aren't we going to Scorpious's base?"

Ernest said " Osirus! Are you dumb or what man? Scorpious's base is close to a Kashmir village so of course in Kashmir !"

"Ok," said Osirus.

Then Osirus was waiting for Shaun to Bath. After a few minutes, Osirus went to bathe. He brushed his teeth, then washed with Hot water, as for him it's great. He felt the Satisfaction In his whole body, his skin becoming hot and producing steam like cooked food and the hot bubbles popping. Even though he likes hot water, he doesn't like extremely hot water which can burn skin or hurt, He likes medium hot water which is hot, but not too hot, but not cold either. The water he took was a little hotter than his category but he felt good bathing and felt like he should stay in there, he came out with steam in his whole body as if he came out of an explosion. His hair was wet, he wore a towel and then wore clothes. He wore the same black shirt, a Brown jacket, dark blue cargo pants, the same sharp belt, and even, the same white Snickers. Even though the jacket and stuff were the same, he wore different ones, like he had duplicates of them, kinda weird, but only the belt was of the Diwali celebration. They had plans for Diwali celebrations, but because of Assassin's the three of Them can't celebrate Diwali.

Then Osirus combed his hair with an electronic comb, and he was prepared to leave.

Shaun had also prepared to wear a White T-shirt, Dark red Jacket, and Black Jeans.

Ernest also prepared himself wearing a grey shirt with buttons, with the sleeves of the shirt folded, and a black jacket on top, Dark green Cargo, He then said "Let's leave take your bags, phones, and everything."

They took everything and decided to go through Shaun's car, as it's faster, has energy, has better battery life, better speed, smoothness, and has strong glass that is made strong to protect from strong things. Still, it's not too strong if bullets are shot

something sharp is thrown extreme power is used or the car crashes, etc. They started the Car and Shaun was driving it. He was driving it, They were listening to music and talking.

Two Hours Went By and It was 8 AM, they went out of Delhi and Entered Haryana state.

They were driving and forgot about the fight and stuff to relax and refresh their mind.

Then Shaun felt something weird like if someone is following them. Then Shaun took the car to a really weird structure site, which looks like it was at a time under construction and seemed to be blacklisted and no one even visited it after being blacklisted. It was waterlogged from the inside and had formed a rectangular hole with water in it, probably because of heavy rains from many years.

Osirus asked, " Why did you stop the car ?"

Shaun said, "I want to show you guys something come inside there". He took the bag and removed the box for which the Assassins had been looking for.

Shaun said "This is the box, they had been looking for, Osirus, This box contains the powers of the previous Assassin who died because of that attack, it's their old leader's powers which are powerful and if they Get it, it's gonna be hard to defeat them and that's why we are going to Scorpious's base.

"Oh, that's the reason they are trying to kill us for the box and you want to show it to me." Said Osirus.

Then Ernest asked, " But Shaun, why did you want to show it now ?"

Shaun said " Because now I felt some sensation of someone following us and it's probably the Assa-"

Suddenly the same fluid kind of energy came but this time it was not thrown but it was coming from the hand of One of the Assassins and it was on the rope pattern, On the back Fourth was written and, he wore a black mask, not only him, all the 6 of them.

This time there was Another Assassin, Bulky 6 feet 9, His long hair flowing, and His mask gave out breath. He had cocked up to a strong Katana. On his back, 5 was written.

Another Assassin out there, with 6 written behind his sleek, his skin Band brown, he stood sternly with no movement into him.

" The six of them came this time," said Ernest.

"Wait, there are six? How many in total?"asked Osirus.

"The primary leaders and other formidable ones make eight, but their army consists of at least 400 Assassins. The eight leaders are the most dangerous," Shaun explained.

"Four hundred? What the hell," said Osirus in shock. "But it looks like there are at least 20 of them! Shit."

"The one with 'Six' written on the back said, 'You pathetic pawns of that old guy are going to die. We asked for the box, but you bastards are trying to be his slaves, bringing in another rascal.'"

Shaun said, " Shut up you assassin, You all only know to discriminate and talk trash, you guys have the craving to die badly."

The Fifth One said, "Now you all are gone, **Sirius**!!" Then the bullets started shooting from the last floor.

From above one of the Assassins fired his A24 rifle. Looked at him, he wore a black sleek, 7 on his back, his skin Olive. He jumped off the floor.

"What!! This Dipshit has come! They are not six but seven" Said Ernest.

Shaun and Ernest conjured a shield using their magical powers to block the bullets, the bullet firing speed and the muzzle flash colour changed from dark yellow to dark bloody red, as if the rifle was already robust and then enhanced with magic. One bullet hit Shaun's leg; it caused pain in the lower limb, the nerves were paining, and the lower limb bone broke, it even went through the whole leg instead of getting stuck like a foreign object. Shaun was in extreme pain, then Sirius, on whose back "Seventh" was written, came down from the floor, stopped firing, and hit the shields of Shaun and Ernest. The other Assassins also attacked.

Osirus stopped watching it and took a sharp fountain pen he had in his pocket to use as a weapon and stabbed it straight in An Assassin's Spine, he was the Fourth Assassin.

The fourth Groaned, "Kill this maniac."

Some assassins came on top of Osirus. Osirus stopped their Kunai with hands and feet and kicked the Fifth Assassin in his Chest, Osirus then kicked the other two Assassins in their face. In contrast, Shaun and Ernest were beating the crap out of the Other Assassins. Ernest caught Sirius's Gun and turned it towards up and the gun fired in the sky, then he kicked him on his waist and then Turned him around and then On his hip, But Sirius Hit Ernest With the upper part of his rifle which was super sharp, which sliced Ernest's left eyebrow's End, causing it to bleed and Sirius applied pressure on the injury so much that Ernest was in extreme pain, the bleeding continued and Sirius hit Ernest with his ankle on Ernest's Jaw.

Then Shaun threw all Assassins to the side. Before Sirius could pull the trigger to shoot Ernest, Shaun came and constantly punched him, until the first Assassin Came and held him by his neck trying to choke Shaun, But Shaun Slammed him in the water. He then kicked the Assassin In his stomach. Then Ernest Kicked Sirius And threw him on a pillar.

The other Assassin's attacked on Osirus. The Second Assassin held Osirus's collar and punched him with force in his face twice, causing blood to come from Osirus's nose. Then he kicked Osirus in his stomach and Punched him in his face, then the fourth Assassin held him back and stabbed the katana in Osirus's stomach. At that very moment, Osirus's Eyes became Huge, and red nerves were seen in his eyes, With a lot of blood coming out then the Assassin took out the katana held Osirus by his collar, and threw him in the water deep.

Shaun Shouted "**No Osirus!**"

Ernest Yelled "**Osirus!!!!**"

The third Assassin said, " That new guy is dead, now you both dumb heads are also gonna face the same fate he faced".

CHAPTER THREE

As they are about to attack. Suddenly, Osirus's eyes opened, The wounds were covered with a violet colour, as if it was healing and the nose bleeding also stopped, The violet-coloured Particles were moving like sparkles. Osirus woke up as if nothing happened.

"What the hell" shrieked The Fifth Assassin "How's that even possible!"

Then The Fourth Assassin spun the Katana in the Air to behead Osirus, but the Katana blade shattered like Glass. Then Osirus held the fourth with his right Fist with ease and Slammed him in the water hard causing big waves of water. He then held the second Assassin's Neck with his left arm, lifted him and threw him on a pillar leading to big cracks causing tremors, and the building could collapse anytime.

Then Shaun Said " Are you Okay Osirus ?" He did not reply but continued to fight the Assassins, and then The first Assassin came.

"Shit" exclaimed Shaun. Then Ernest Jumped and hooked his legs on the first assassin causing the neck of the first to be trapped in between Ernest's legs and performed a backflip to throw the first Assassin into the water, In the process he too fell hard into the Water And then he came to help Osirus in the fight, then Osirus launched a punch on both of them, they dodged... Amidst this, Ernest sensed someone more of an Assassin,

and he said "Oh no! Shaun and Osirus, he has arrived"

Shaun said, "We need to run, Osirus!!"

Osirus replied in a rough voice "Get yourself out of here."

Then came their leader sprinting with around 25 Assassins.

Looking at him, Black robes with a cape, a hood covering his hair, and fair skin. He appeared intimidating and mysterious.

Shaun shouted " Shit! Run Osirus, Ernest!"

They ran but Osirus stood there with the desire to fight them.

Then came the Assassin leader holding a gigantic axe in his arm, having a black Scarf mask donned, covering his lips and nose. Then Osirus or the one who took over him cleared the blood adventuring from his mouth and erected a square-shaped shield, Violet in colour with lustre on it. The leader then caught firm hold of the giant axe and took it a bit back and with speed and brute force, Smacked it hard on the Square-shaped shield, causing trembling in the shield and Osirus's Body.

As the Structure started breaking, The leader said "Alastor (Third Assassin) go and get the box.

Alastor said, "Yes leader."

Then the leader pointed a finger at Sirius and made some signs

"Ok, Javon (Leader) I'll do it." Javon removed his mask. Looked at Javon, His eyes were bloody red, With red nerves in his eyes. He then took the Axe and started breaking the pillars and the other Assassins shot the structure at last the structure collapsed and they teleported.

Meanwhile, the three sat and started the car, but Osirus was in a bad condition and fell unconscious. They checked to see, that Osirus had fallen unconscious on his seat. They realised he was fine, so they drove the car from there ASAP. They even increased their speed by using their powers. The car was going so fast that when it hit the speed bump. The Car went 5 metres up from the ground. Hitting the heads of Shaun, Ernest And Osirus. This caused Osirus to wake up. His eyes had opened with him analysing what was happening.

His heart was pumping blood faster than it was ever, it was bypassing the fat in the arteries with ease.

"What Happened there ?" Asked Osirus in a Low tone.

Ernest spoke in a loud voice and said "You beat the crap out of them, How the hell in this world did you manage to do that? That also without any training !!?"

Osirus was scared to know and yelled "What the hell, I don't have any idea of how I did it, I probably should've not done it."

Shaun said, "Shut up saying bullcrap of '*I should've not done it*', you did the right thing and stop talking trash now, you just downplaying yourself !!!"

As The car's speed was high, They had to drive in inappropriate ways. Causing Police behind them.

"Ayo, the Police are coming after us!" Shouted Osirus.

"Holy s-" Said Shaun in a loud voice.

They increased the car's speed to such an extent that the roads could not be used to track the car's location properly as the trail of the car was inconsistent.

They were trying to relax and stopped the car on a thick mountain road.

"Oh no, even the police were behind us" Said Osirus, "But they have seen the number plate, we are so done for now".

Shaun Said " Don't worry Kid, I had put a black tape before you came running and made sure no proof is left behind."

As they were taking a deep breath, Shaun and Osirus Sensed Something, Shaun could sense it strongly only to realise that Alastor, The Third Assassin was there on the top of the jungle trees.

Osirus Exclaimed "Shit !!!, Shaun !!"

Shaun used his powers again to increase the speed and drove it out from there. Alastor jumped on the road and then started running behind the car with a katana in the hands. He was running so fast that he had almost caught up to the swiftness of a car.

Osirus Loudly Exclaimed, "Shaun, Drive faster !!!!!"

Then Alastor jumped in the car and made it to the Car's rear end, then jumped to the front and made it to the driver's door, then he tried putting the Katana in Shaun's Neck. But Shaun Pressed the lever causing his seat to go down swiftly.

Ernest Stopped The Katana and Pushed It outside. Shaun used his left Leg to use the steering wheel for driving And Punched Alastor which caused him to Go back to where Osirus was.

Osirus got scared. Ernest Shouted And Said " Osirus !! Punch !!!".

Osirus was scared and thought that it was the right decision to hit him in the face.

Shaun said "Punch Him He's the one who killed your fa-"

Osirus then punched Alastor In his Face.

Shaun then took his leg off the wheel and began driving like an ordinary person, and Told Ernest " Ernest, Go and

Beat the crap out of him quickly."

Before he could Attack Osirus Again Ernest Kicked Him on his face. Causing him To fall from the Car.

"Arse Assassin." Said Osirus "Wait but how could he kill him, he's pretty young, how could Assassins age that slow."

"No, I just tried pissing you over so that you fight and it worked... oh no the car."

Shaun Struggled to drive fast and control the car properly Simultaneously.

Then Alastor jumped again but this time on the roof trying to stab the Katana in them. The Katana Pierced through the roof And Fortunately, Ernest Held The Katana which could've likely killed him. Alastor took the Katana back.

Ernest's hand was bleeding and there was a slice on it.

He felt a bit of pain, but the slice was healing slowly.

Then Shaun Started driving with hands And then

Alastor again Stabbed the Katana which had the possibility of ripping Shaun's ear off, but fortunately, Shaun went on his side.

Then Ernest Opened the car door and went on the car roof to face Alastor.

Then Alastor tried punching Ernest, But he dodged it and held it. Alastor tried stabbing the Katana but Ernest Held the other arm as well and Hit Him with a Leg on the jaw. Then Ernest was again attacked with a Katana but this time his veins turned blue, consumed in vengeance he burned the Katana and threw it. The whole thing turned into nothing but Ashes.

Alastor then took out a Kunai knife from His Pocket and attempted to impale it in Ernest's Face. But, he failed to do so and tried Impaling it in Ernest's Left knee joint but, Ernest Stopped the kunai and Head butted him On his head. Then Alastor Kicked Ernest And then He Jumped on the roof and positioned himself as If he was trying to have balance on the roof too. But He Impaled the Kunai on the roof in an attempt to kill Osirus Or Shaun. The Impaled Kunai Pierced through the Roof creating a hole. Fortunately Enough, It did not Hit Osirus. Osirus was shocked to see that and screamed in agony and a weird way as if he was crying " Why !??, Ernest Can't you just kill him quick!!".

Shaun said, "Ernest Be careful!! I will come".

Then Ernest Kicked Alastor in his face and held his neck and tried throwing him but Somehow! He still managed to remain on the Roof. He removed the mask he had worn he had a cut with blood close to his lips and kept the mask inside one of the pockets. Then Alastor Tried Hitting him Again but Ernest Finally Stopped his Hand Heated the Kunai A bit then kicked his arm. Causing the Kunai to fall down the mountain.

Then Alastor Hit Ernest with punches and Kicked him In the face and Then Alastor pulled out the last weapon, his gun from his pocket. Suddenly Ernest came running towards him but then swiftly He loaded the Gun and Pulled the trigger and from the gun, in 2 seconds 4 bullets flew out of the gun barrel And hit Ernest's chest consecutively on both sides of His chest passing through various artilleries, Then he fired the rest beneath the car roof.

Shaun said, "What the - Ernest!!"

Osirus Screamed "Ernest!!!!!".

The bullet shells were tumbling down on the road. Ernest's chest was bleeding. His eyes went white And Was about to go Unconscious. Alastor Replenished the Gun magazine and Pointed at Ernest's Skull. Then Ernest's eyes Opened Up. But They were Light blue, Ernest Seemed to be in a conscious State And then in his fists, a Blade Got

Forged up, Then Ernest Flew His fist and Split up the Gun. Cutting off the front side and the Barrel Of the Pistol. Then Ernest Swung his Arm in the Air and Stabbed The Blade in Alastor's Scapula which ended up breaking His Scapula as well as the Clavicle and broke the whole Joint Then Ernest deftly extracted the blade embedded in Alastor's shoulder and went Inside Car's backseat Where Osirus Was Shocked and Scared. Then Alastor Jumped on the car's Window and His hands were like a blade, sharp enough to pierce through a human's body. Then Ernest Had a lot of Blue aura dripping around and Covering his body translucently and glowing lustrous, Then Ernest Punched Alastor Hard on his chest cracking up his ribcage, He still Managed a grip he was extremely Injured but he still had the desire to attain the Box.

Then Ernest Spoke in a fast tone "Pen !!, Pen !!, Pen!!" and shouted out loudly "Osirus!!"

"Here !" said Osirus "I got you".

Then Ernest Stabbed it In Alastor's heart, piercing the cardiac muscles. A small sprinkle of blood which looked like water leakage sprinkled. Then Ernest took Out the Pen and stabbed it in his Neck and Then Alastor's Hand Started Loosening and Bleeding, Gasping for breath kicked in & Ernest transferred extreme heat to burn Alastor's body, with the gasping stopping, Skin becoming like dirty leather and then Alastor Was no longer on the Car and at The CREEDS base, murdered. With Assassin's Gathered looking at the corpse Of Alastor.......

CHAPTER FOUR

AfterAlastor Was dead, Shaun stopped the car because After the huge fight all of them were tired and Ernest was severely injured and in a really bad condition. He Came out of the car and Sat close to a Tyre.

Osirus asked, "Ernest !!, are you okay ?"

Ernest replied in a low tone "Yeah, I'm okay".

Then Shaun came out of the car running.

Then he asked, " Ernest, what happened are you feeling like you need help for recovery."

Ernest answered, " Nah, no, it's healing."

Then all of Ernest's veins appeared but they were blue And then The four Bullets came out and Blood also stopped dripping out from the chest.

Ernest's 6 ribs were broken and they were slowly recovering.

Then Osirus Asked " Shaun, When the hell !! will we get secure?."

Shaun replied, "Pretty soon."

Osirus then shouted and asked Shaun "How the hell can they be so powerful and durable in combat and here we are lacking against them in hand-to-hand combat how are we gonna adjust this."

Shaun replied, "Then the only thing we have to do is reach Scorpious's base as fast as possible."

Osirus then again asked a bit angrily "What if they get the box then what are you gonna do."

Shaun answered, "We will go and get the box and if required I'll kill those Scumbags even if I'll have to die."

Then Ernest stood up and said, " Now let's go already."

Osirus said shockingly " What the, you recovered so fast." replied in a friendly manner " Hehh, yeah we developed it but wait let the ribs recover only 3 are located back and joint ."

Ater a few minutes Ernest recovered and took a deep breath.

Then the three of them started talking. But as they were talking close to a tree Sirius was holding his A24 rifle. On it, **Creeds** was carved. He then pulled the charging handle for the bullets to get Prepared.

As soon as the lever was pulled. Osirus, Shaun, and Ernest heard it.

Osirus panicked and screamed, " frick!!!! Run start the frickin car!!!!!!".

And Sirius pulled the trigger and fired bullets, fortunately, The bullets hit the car. Then Shaun Started The car and drove it fast and enhanced the speed. Then Sirius Jumped and Started flying at the Speed of a Car simultaneously Firing.

"What the!" Snapped Osirus.

Then unexpectedly and surprisingly Shaun Kept his left arm up and Quickly blue energy was generated and his Nails became sharp as Huge Energy went through and hit Sirius but He didn't lose track instead he gained speed and came back at full throttle. The Energy blast that Shaun had there didn't blow up the roof and didn't impact Sirius that much, he came in front of the car And pulled the trigger and it fired bullets in such energy that the glass in front got cracked and the bullet went till the backseat. Fortunately, Enough It didn't hit Osirus.

Then Ernest Held Sirius And caught hold of the gun And threw it but Sirius swiftly switched to a machete and tried stabbing it, Ernest Threw him behind and there Sirius Stabbed Osirus On his Left humerus causing it to bleed and Osirus fell Unconscious, Sirius took the Machete out and tried stabbing it to Ernest But Ernest Kicked Sirius and Threw him down the mountain.

Sirius was falling down but then Sirius took a powerful flight and came back and caught up to the speed of the car But then Ernest had a Pistol and Shot all the bullets out. One of the bullets hit Sirius in the middle of his chest but the bullet came out and fell behind. Then Sirius took another powerful flight and sliced an Eagle's Left wing and made it to the window where Shaun's driving. Ernest was loading the gun when Sirius removed his mask, opened his Maw And threw some power out, Ernest and Shaun crouched down to dodge the attack, Ernest Dodged it but Shaun got a minor burn on his parietal. Osirus Woke up in the meanwhile.

Then Shaun Punched Sirius on his chest But He didn't leave.

Then Shaun asked Osirus "Gimme the Pen Osirus quick".

Osirus threw him the pen.

Then Shaun said, " See this is the blood of that other Scumbag who's now a Dead body I will show you rewind". Pointed Finger At Ernest "Of how he killed him."

Sirius said " You son of a-"

Then Shaun stabbed the Pen Consecutively in Sirius's Heart 5 times and fell off the road.

Then Shaun kept the pen in his mouth like a cigar which he could throw if anyone came.

Sirius Woke up and started walking like a zombie. His left leg was broken and dislocated.

Osirus was in a really bad condition. His wound was not healing quickly.

Ernest shouted "Osirus !!" and then said, "Try recovering".

Osirus said in pain and irritation "What the hell are you saying Ernest, I Am here stabbed and you are telling me to recover by myself !!"

Ernest then said "Sorry mate, just hold on".

Ernest Helped Osirus in Healing. The wound started Packing up, the Skin was stitched up and the blood stopped dripping.

Osirus said in a low tone "Crap the jacket is spoilt, I'll have to wash it".

In the meanwhile Sirius's leg jerked up and recovered and then again Started flying and caught up to the speed of the car.

" Ah shit, here we go again, That moron's coming again." Gagged Shaun.

Osirus said, "Oh come on, how are they so damn strong, You guys are vulnerable."

Ernest then replied, "Oh, so if we are vulnerable, then you were Supposed to be dead in Delhi, Use your brain o contemplate not your knees."

Osirus was silent.

Then Sirius Went on the roof and impaled the Machete through the roof and almost stabbed through Shaun's skull but Shaun swiftly shifted his head from there just in the neck of time. Then Sirius took Out the Machete and Impaled it backside of the roof where Osirus was Sitting.

He impaled but Osirus swiftly moved his skull as well but was not swifter than Shaun and Osirus 's forehead got slit. Blood started coming from that narrow opening.

Osirus Said in pain "Ah Crap."

Sirius moved the Machete a bit But Osirus went down his seat to prevent getting stabbed.

Then Ernest Closed His eyes and Said "Osirus!, Put your arms on your ears and close your eyes."

Then Ernest drew off his pistol and loaded the magazine and cocked the pistol. Then he aimed it sloping his arms upwards and then Ernest Pulled the trigger and the Bullet came out and went through the car roof and struck straight at Sirius's Head. The gunshot fired wasn't any Ordinary. Ernest used his powers to boost the impact and damage of the bullet. The shell swung in Speed and went outside the road.

Then Ernest fired Consecutively 3 times in the same direction.

Shaun felt a bit wobbly in his ears. Osirus couldn't

Hear a thing temporarily.

Sirius's skull got a crack and he fell from the roof on the road. But The Bullet was slowly coming forth.

The Bullet dropped on the road, the bullet mark was vanishing. Then Sirius started chasing the car again as if nothing happened and then He Took a huge flight and started chasing the car again and then His nails got sharpened and looked like claws and then he pierced through the air and put his hand in the ripped hole, there was the A24 rifle. Sirius cocked the rifle and placed it on full Auto mode and Pulled the trigger. The bullets were fired and they pierced through the car roof. The bullets were also more powerful because Sirius used his powers to make the bullets more effective.

The rounds were already finished but the bullets were still coming out as Sirius produced more bullets with his powers. Ernest drew out a protective covering around the car. Even though it was deflecting the bullets, the covering also had some damage. Then Sirius flew at extreme speed and again his Hand was mutating and they became like those claws he used to create a portal to get the gun but this time he Struck the Car With those nails causing in breaking the protective covering.

Ernest in Frustration said, "Holy shit, he broke open the Shield."

Then Osirus snatched the Bag from Ernest took out his Home knife drew out the box a bit, pointed the Knife towards the box and then shouted "I'll freaking stab in this stupid Shitty box ."

Sirius Seemed to be affected but then he seemed like he did not hesitate and then He pointed the Gun at Osirus. Removed the Mag out from the Gun reloaded it with bullets Inserted it back, and Pulled the charging handle.

Then Osirus Said, "H-hey, I will Destroy it."

Then Shaun Held the Gun Firmly with his Fist And then Sirius used his Other arm to close His Fist with only The index and middle finger out and then Placed the Fingers below Shaun's jaw.

Shaun Replied, "What the fish".

Sirius Tilted his two fingers placed beneath The jaw breaking Shaun's Full Jaw, Making Shaun unable to speak. The Jaw was Displaced. The car started going in an erratic path.

Then Ernest Tried shooting Sirius but then He formed a rope, Caught hold of Ernest's neck and tied the Rope at his seat.

Then Osirus Exclaimed, "Ya screwed up Now".

But then Sirius Held Osirus's Knife and Dropped It on the Car's floor and Caught Hold Of the Box and tried Snatching The Box But then Osirus Also Held the Box Firmly and tried Pulling it towards himself.

Sirius Then Formed A Small Stick and tried Poking it Into Osirus's Eye. It Caused Osirus To lose Grip of the Box And he fell on his seat.

And unfortunately, which is Fortunate for The Assassins, Sirius Got The box and He went out of the Car, Shot The Back Tyre of the car and fled away. The car crashed into a Huge Rock which then Toppled it on the ground. It Broke The Windows of the car, and the glass pieces got impaled In Osirus's Neck and Close to the eye. All of them Were Unconscious and hit by broken glass.

CHAPTER FIVE

The car was all Broken. Osirus was lying injured and Unconscious just like Ernest. Shaun Was Inside there too, but unlike Osirus and Ernest, he was conscious. He had the Seatbelt holding him inside the car. He Took off the seatbelt And tried waking up the two.

Meanwhile, Javon and all the Assassins were all collected in groups with a lot of them and In between Was the Burning box in which Alastor's body was being Cremated. The box was made of metal, with Alastor's Spear on the box with his Katana and Gun not found.

Javon was there standing. No one had a tear or feeling of loss as if nothing happened.

Then Javon said, "Alastor The Third Assassin's dead, because of his weakness, he couldn't get a Box which is important for our growth he deserves this death and I guess Sirius's dead probably, if he is dead that wouldn't make things any more disappointing then that."

Then someone raised his arm. Everyone looked at him, It was Sirius who had returned with the box.

Sirius said "Javon!!, I bought the Box, now we can destroy that nuisance old Guy and those bunch of nuisance."

Javon said, "Magnificent, You didn't disappoint me at least." Then exclaimed, "(sigh) And you Bastards can't even take down one amateur, come on at least not those experienced Morons, kill that One amateur whatever the hell his experience is or at least catch him you fools can't even do that!, Pass me the gun ."

Then Javon Shot two of the Assassins in the liver. One of them reacted to the damage and felt pain. The Assassin groaned as his mask revealed his face in agony.

Then Javon shouted and shot him in the head and blew up that Assassin's Skull, the amateur Assassin Collapsed to his death. Then Javon yelled "Another Weak Arse!!"

Then Sirius Asked, "I did the task victoriously, but will I get any of the part of the Powers?"

Javon then conveyed "Of course, You will get the powers but first, I have to break it damn open 'cause this box's opening requires time". Then grumbled "I wish that stupid **'Harsh'** should've Died in the air before captivating the powers.'

Then Javon commanded to everyone "Everyone will now start preparing and will increase the security level to make sure that those Three or whoever the hell comes should not even enter and die By thinking of our security, you all will begin from now!!"

Everyone said "Yes Leader !!!!!, we'll not disappoint you."

Meanwhile, Ernest came back to consciousness and both of them tried waking Osirus up. Osirus looked severely injured and there were some cuts on his neck and face. Ernest tried performing chest compressions, but suddenly Osirus woke up.

Osirus Then Said, "Shaun Your Jaw's okay ?"

Shaun then Mumbled a bit "Itsh a bit fine and Itsh betta now and Itsh slowly recovering ish will take shum time."

Osirus Then Said, "Why the Hell are ya talking like An alcoholic."

Shaun then mumbled, "How za fudge do you Know zat an Alcoholic specs like dis."

Osirus said, "Come on no one with a broken jaw speaks like that, only a frickin alcoholic speaks like this !"

Ernest then said, "Idiots, where the box is gone and you are fighting like cats, stop dis bullshit."

Osirus shouted "What!! you guys didn't Stop that guy, even when he was there in the car before crashing."

Then Ernest said, "He frickin tied my throat with rope, broke Shaun's Jaw and how do you expect us to stop him even when the car crashed, now it's to be fixed."

Osirus then Said, "(sigh) Btw Guys, when are we starting the training as the car will take some time to repair."

Ernest then conveyed "Well that's a nice idea, even though it won't take much time but we can train for a bit of time I mean 48 hours ."

Shaun Then mumbled and questioned, "Then who is gonna repair da kar ?"

Osirus and Ernest then replied, "You, 'cause we aren't that shiny in Engineering so you, plus you are the rich-ass jacked guy so again *you*."

Osirus then said, "If you guys couldn't protect that box, then what's the point of me training and us repairing the car it's over."

"Not really." Said Ernest.

"Huh?"

Shaun then mumbled, "Shey will take some time to Ospen da Box Sho we can strain you to at least kick one or two asses and I am going to take some time."

Osirus asked "Okay, But I Had One Question, Do you guys know those Assassin's history and their names."

Ernest replied, "Yeah we do know, but why do you want to know ?"

Osirus then said "Just curiosity.....Of course, I have to know, they nearly ended my life!"

Ernest then replied, "(sigh) Fine I'll tell you, (takes a long gap), now listen up The Assassin group we are fighting are called the **Creeds**."

Osirus Said, "I frickin know it that they are called Creeds & they are B tier".

Ernest Then continued "(chuckles) Oh yeah! Okay lemme continue so the guy that Shaun Threw at the trash bin is **Jules**, the first Assassin, even though he is the least powerful you can't easily sense his presence, but it's not as difficult as it sounds still, he is a pretty tough guy. The second guy is **Atlantas**, he is the second one, well he is even tougher like even though Alastor is in a better position, just because of this Scumbag's less speed, **Alastor** is ranked higher or else he is better than **Alastor** In agility and at somewhat level strength than The Third Assassin is..... actually-y was **Alastor**, he is the Third Assassin -."

Osirus then Interrupted and spoke sarcastically "Yeah like if you didn't tell me, of course you told me about him during Ya were telling me about That Altantic-Atlantas or Somethin."

Ernest then said, "Oh fine then, so yeah Alastor, well he was pretty strong and fast but as you know he is dead, so let's move, The next one is **Bludreth ."**

Osirus then asked, "So that means you are saying the names from 1-8 and the 8ᵗʰ one is a leader."

Ernest replied "Y-yeah ." Then continued "Bludreth is not a great deal but will make you wet your pants."

"Okay, I bear it 'cause that's all I can do." Said Osirus.

Ernest then Said, "Ugh just listen now, So the Next's **Thraxor**, He has a lot of Brutalities and he can use Heavy weapons pretty well and can use Knives pretty skillfully as well and he is swifter than Alastor he will slit your throat even before ya realising and the next one's **Sangorath**, you are not gonna be having an advantage over this Asshole, he's *literal*Monster, he can be considered a literal Genocide, even if you are dead he will keep on Impaling, destroying you until the Leader doesn't hesitate, (Sigh) well it doesn't even sound that intimidating to us now there's even worse."

Osirus looked scared and said "Holy What !, it gets even brutal, now are the other two Cannib-."

Ernest said "Nah!! , but still dangerous, well the next one is **Sirius**, he was the One who was firing A24 and took away that box, he's way too powerful he will reduce you to atoms and make you feel pain and yeah he's the most experienced in wielding Firearms, he is crazy experienced in operating Firearms and his aim is also pretty dangerous even though he wasn't able to kill us because we made it difficult for him to shoot at us as he kept on getting shot but he is nothing in front of the leader, his name is... *Javon,* who's the most vicious, wild and the most menacing out of them, will first Capture you, drain out every single bit of energy and then he will kill you brutally, he is unpredictable In what way he kills anyone, he has killed many Of his own Assassin's ."

Shaun conveyed "(relived) My jaw's okay now, It still makes my Jaw hurt and makes it Red and feels like friction is caused in my jaw but yeah I'm okay, crap it hurts, so Basically all of them are Bloodlusts, blood thirsts, wild, vehement and what else no one knows."

Osirus then Asked shockingly "How the hell in this world do you guys know all this stuff !!".

Ernest replied, "I guess you shouldn't know it, at least for now."

Osirus then asked, "Now I am curious, speak out !?".

Ernest Then said in a loud tone "I'll tell you later, chill !"

Osirus then said in a low tone "(Sigh) Fine."

Then Ernest and Shaun took Osirus for training somewhere at an abandoned place.

There Osirus asked, "What am I gonna learn first?"

Ernest then asked, "Do you know combat?"

Osirus replied, "(nervous) Yeah-yeah, of course, I am the mother- I-I mean the father of combat."

Shaun then interjected, "Meh, that was cringe we understood you are decent or somewhat something in combat now try fighting."

Then Ernest formed two sticks in both arms and tossed one of the sticks to Osirus.

Then Ernest said "You are good in combat right ?" then continued "So try hitting me consecutively 5 times it must be easy for you, right ?"

Osirus itching and grinning head said, "Y-yeah, I guess.."

Then Ernest said, "You better be good 'cause the attacks are gonna be very strong."

Osirus then stammered "(nervous) Yeah-yeah I am okay."

Ernest then replied "(Sigh) Fine let's start.

Osiris had sweat dripping from his forehead... In his mind "Holy moly! , How will I defeat Ernest."

Then Ernest Held the stick firmly and sprinted towards Osirus. Then Osirus flew the stick from his right hand towards Ernest, it was about to hit Ernest on his jaw but Ernest caught hold of the stick and hit Osirus under the arm and then knocked him on the stomach.

Osirus was in pain with his intestines being wobbly, he fell on the ground with his anal muscles absorbing the shock and then said "Ah crap, it hurts I feel pain in my Intestines" Then further stated, "Even my hips hurt ah.. crap!!."

Ernest being embarrassed, said in a low tone "Wow, how did I forget that he got beaten up by the Assassins without him doin' anything."

Osirus Then replied, "Because You were frickin sayin like if I didn't knew you'll eat me."

Ernest then exclaimed in a bit annoyance "But why do you have to lie !, If you had told me this would not have happened." Then said, " (Sigh) now let's start the training ."

Then Osirus stood up and caught hold of his stick again.

Ernest Then said "Focus Properly make sure that you can Hit me and make it hurt for a while" and then said "A.. and make sure that Anti-genosis doesn't take over ya."

Osirus was confused and burst out laughing "What the hell." then said, "Why does he have such a nasty name."

Ernest Then replied, "Hey, don't mess with him he's too strong and he's the one who rescued you from the mouth of Yama himself."

Osirus then said, "Nah they are not yama but they felt like they were from hell."

Ernest then shouted, "Now start learning!!"

Osirus was alarmed and then said, "O-kkk-ok let's start !!"

Then Osirus moved in full force to Hit Ernest on his belly. Osirus was About to hit Ernest when he departed from his place and Hit Osirus on his spine. Osirus felt it, the affliction made his nerves & spine shiver and there Osirus fell hard on the ground.

Ernest then said, "Can you handle this." Then exclaimed "No! Right! , then why come runnin'."

Osirus in agony says "I was just tryna attack ya."

Ernest then shouted, "Now listen to what I say!"

Osirus was irritated "Ugh, fine now let's start."

Shaun's dad started working to repair the car.

Meanwhile, Javon Was attempting to wide open the box. He was trying every way he could think of opening.

Javon in anger said, "(Sigh) Ugh.. damn it, it's not opening, it's taking so long."

Then Sirius came in and asked, "Javon, when are you gonna give me the powers of the box".

Javon then replied angrily "Are you dull-witted, can't you frickin see that I am trying to open this thing."

Sirius said, "Oh my bad, but make sure I get a part of it forget about that Sangorath I want my part ."

Javon then said, "**I will** now don't keep on asking it time and again, talk about it when it's the time."

Sirius replied "(sigh) Fine, but you make sure I get it or else you'll know what I am ."

Javon then exclaimed and said "What the hell do you mean I'll know you? Do you want to know me? You didn't do any favour to me by bringing this thing I told you I'll give you then now shut up."

Sirius then said, "Forget that you don't wanna know that."

Sirius walks out of the room.

Javon whispers "Bastard."

On the Other hand, Osirus was contemplating What in peanut butter hell is he doing with his life.

Ernest Said "Take this stick and Try hitting me, I am not using my Powers I'll teach you while fighting ."

Osirus Said "Are you sure, I should fight you?"

Ernest said, "Just take the damn!! stick and come and attempt hitting me with it ".

Osirus then Irritated Said, "Ugh, fine."

Ernest Threw the Stick and Osirus caught it.

Ernest then snapped, "Come at me."

Osirus asserted, "K."

Then Osirus caught Sprint with the uttermost speed he could get and Was All on the purpose of Hitting Ernest.

Then Ernest displaced himself From his Position caught Hold Of Osirus clasped his jacket and then exclaimed "You Should Attack Now!!!"

Then Osirus Swung his stick But Ernest Booted Osirus's leg Causing him to fall Ernest caught hold of his Arm and placed the Stick on His throat.

Then Osirus Kicked Ernest successfully, and it landed causing Ernest to roll up on the side Osirus Hit the Stick firmly on Ernest's face causing the zygomatic bone part of the skin of Ernest to swell a bit and become red.

Ernest in pain whispered "(gasps) Ahh shit" then conveyed and shouted "Nice Strike but ... *now take this!!*"

Then He booted Osirus on the Chest Causing Osirus to be Knocked out and then Ernest Stood Up trembling and then Took a long gasp.

Osirus Then questioned in Agony "Ahh crap, why you ain't Attacking, aren't you supposed to be Hostile towards your enemies?"

Ernest then replied, "Yeah, But you should take a resting breath as well to relieve yourself in a fight, I would fight constantly if the opponent is tough and can cause a problem and you are anything but a tough opponent ."

Osirus Irritated hearing it stood up swiftly and ran towards Ernest and took his right leg towards Ernest's face to kick it to blow off a hit on the face but Ernest caught hold of the right Leg and threw Osirus On the ground hard.

Osirus Could feel the pain In his nerves, spine, and Whole body in short especially in the Right Leg's thigh. So much that his whole body was shivering, and his right leg was paralyzed, he could barely move it.

Osirus in Physical agony "ah... Crap, it hurts so Frickin Bad."

Ernest said, "You should control yourself even in anger, Know how to use that damn aggression."

Osirus Then Grumbled, "Shut up, stop talking like a wise Philosopher or something."

Ernest then Protested "Me, talking like a wise Philosopher ?? Huh? Then well *I am* ."

Meanwhile, both of them were fighting like cats Shaun was busy repairing the car.

He sighed "(Sigh) It's taking time" and then shouted, "Damn a lot of time!!!!".

On the other hand, Osirus is Learning to fight and control his powers with Ernest. Whereas Shaun was Busy repairing the car.

Finally, At 7 PM, Osirus and Ernest stopped their "Special Training".

Ernest shouted, "Shaun, Stop the work and come to eat."

Shaun asked boomingly "What's on the menu"

Ernest replied loudly "Chole".

Shaun then happily said "Nice man ! (realized)" then grumbled "Nooo!! man not again, they taste like-"

A few moments later, Shaun, Osirus and Ernest sat with Chole. "Ready to eat Chole." Took the chole in hand, because no Bhature was there and put it in their mouth

Then Shaun Said with satisfaction "Wow, it tastes good" Then asked "But where is the Bhatura."

Ernest replied "I didn't find ready-to-eat Bhatura-"

Osirus Interrupting said "It tastes good man, Tastes better than the food made at "my Uncle's" home." Then conveyed "It was trash, I would rather eat a human-"

Then Ernest exclaimed, "Ayo, that's cannibalism".

Osirus then muttered, "Yeah yeah whatever."

Then they continued Eating the moderately flavoured, spicy Ball of Chole. Later on, Osirus and Ernest continued training till midnight only to sleep. meanwhile, Shaun was busy repairing the demolished car.

CHAPTER SIX

It was 3 AM dawn, and the sky was dark purple, with barely any sunlight, pretty much the whole world was asleep, including Osirus, who had already been tired from his training, but he did improve his combat, now he could at least do a thing or two to the hundreds of assassins. Ernest also had an hour's nap after all the training he gave to Osirus. His sleep cycle is ruined. But somehow, he still manages to look normal.

Meanwhile, Shaun who is wide awake, is constantly repairing the car severely wrecked by Sirius. It was difficult because the car exterior was damaged and the parts required to drive the vehicle. But Shaun had almost got there, car was nearly repaired.

Shaun who required sleep was tired with pain in his spine and legs stopped the work, contemplating why is he doing this, the only thing he was doing in servicing his car was pain, back pain. Now Shaun will pay his car mechanic better, realizing how messed up it is to repair one car.

Meanwhile, Osirus woke up. He looked like an absolute Geek, under his eyes were dark circles not very visible.

Osirus who slept in some shade came walking, sighting Shaun repairing the car and then called him out "Shaun, is it done?"

Shaun then sarcastically replied, "Yes! it goes so fast that it will crash like the Rs6!"

Osirus exclaimed "Really!"

Shaun replied, "Of course not dumbo, use your eyes it's still left."

Osirus then reacted "Oh" then Said, "Continue."

Shaun then conveyed "Thanks!"

Meanwhile, Ernest shouted "Osirus!"

Osirus asked loudly "What?"

Ernest said "Come for training"

Osirus in his mind thought even why does he have to train in such darkness, at 3 AM?

Then Osirus Walked tired of Ernest. Who was located 30 metres away.

Osirus was confused and asked "Seriously! Now!"

Then Ernest conveyed "Yes of course then why would I frickin call you?"

Osirus then was like "(Sigh........) fine, now let's begin."

Ernest Cracked all his fingers and then landed a punch on Osirus's left cheek causing him to collapse down hard.

"What on earth was that!" Said Osirus in agony.

Then Ernest kicked him in the chest.

"Frickin, stop!" he shouted again.

Then Osirus stood swiftly and Jump-kicked Ernest but, he Stopped the leg before it landed and then he pushed Osirus and Punched him Hard again this time on the chin.

Osirus With Pain then hit Ernest swiftly On his chest, causing Minimal to no damage to Ernest.

"(Gasps) That hurts (Gasps again) doesn't it?" Asked Osirus.

Then Ernest said, "Nope, not a bit, even paper cut hurts more than your attacks."

Then Osirus Shouted out "Damnn You..."

Ernest punched Osirus hard in the face causing him to fall like a broken corpse with no bones.

Osirus was now frustrated and landed A Strong punch on Ernest's Face. The punch was so hard that Ernest felt itchy on his face.

Ernest then complimented "Nice punch my guy Keep it u-" Osirus kicked him hard on the chest.

Then Shouted Osirus like a child "Yes!!! I caught you off guard."

He Kicked Ernest on his abdomen causing Ernest to roll in the air and collapse hard on the ground.

Now Ernest felt hurt.

Ernest whispered slowly "Damn, that hurts a lot."

Ernest quickly stood up, only to be welcomed by a strong piercing kick by Osirus but had barely any impact on Ernest. He Punched Osirus Hard in the face.

Now Osirus got hurt terribly and Ernest Punched him thrice On his stomach and hit him with his Elbow joint hard, causing him to flip and fall hard on the ground.

Osirus when collapsed hard, got a deep cut on his hand, ended up bleeding.

"Tourniquet!!" he screamed "Ernest, I need a Tourniquet for this!"

Ernest Saw the cut and realized it's as much of a cut as you get from a paper.

"Just wash it and you are not even bleeding that much." He said

Well, the bleeding wasn't at least like a river.

I guess Osirus eats his Broccoli.

Then Ernest wondered if his cuts and heavy wounds be healed by his Powers. He saw that his wound was healing slowly.

Then Osirus said "This wound is healing fast" and questioned, "What's happening!?"

"Your healing factor is working" conveyed Ernest.

"What's that, is it like healing fast and I have powers." Asked Osirus.

"Exactly," said Ernest.

"Woah, that's cool." Exclaimed Osirus "But does it matter."

Then Ernest hit his head Hard "Why does he have to say this." He wondered.

Then Ernest Kicked Osirus on the chest hard and Osirus fell off 5 metres away.

Then Osirus extremely frustrated, Stood swiftly and charged a punch towards Ernest only for it to be held and dodged by Ernest and then kicked in the chin causing Osirus to fall in agony.

Then the fight between the two continued for 5 Minutes only to end when Osirus landed a punch on Ernest's Belly and was successful but his arm was caught up and flipped hard. Causing Osirus to be Immobilized for 2 Minutes.

"I can't Move!" Shouted Osirus.

"(Sigh) I guess I didn't hold back enough". Said Ernest in a Low tone.

"You hold back what! That's holding back !" Shouted Osirus.

Then Osirus after 2 minutes was finally able to move his body without feeling pain. Then he stood up and asked, "(Gasps) how long have we been fighting?"

Ernest said, "For 55 minutes and it's 3:55 AM right now."

Osirus then exclaimed "55 Minutes !!! , Woah I didn't know while fighting time passes that fast."

Ernest then conveyed "It does pass fast but not every time, it depends ." Then said

"If the fight is boring or dangerous then it will go slow but if the fight's fun and you are at the lead it will go fast as when we get to experience the good part it passes fast."

Osirus Then said "(Gasps) Right."

Then Ernest was about to take a sprint but Osirus Jerked a heavy Punch At him. Before he could Sprint at a considerable distance, he fell hard on the ground.

Osirus Kicked Ernest on the chest Causing Him to wake up and pop his eyes open as if he had a lucid nightmare and was drowning.

Then Osirus Pushed his leg more with force on the chest, leaving Ernest in Pain But then He Kicked Osirus hard on his butt with the left leg getting out of the hold of him and then Kicked him on his Jaw, Causing Him to spit out Blood and collapse on the ground.

"Oh, Crap !" Reacted Ernest in Shock and fear.

Osirus had collapsed With blood flowing from his mouth. He had almost gone unconscious.

"Ar-re you okay ?" Asked Ernest in fear.

"(In pain) Yeah !! (Panting) I can legit run faster than Usain Bolt in this condition." Exclaimed Osirus Sarcastically.

"Of course not Idiot!" Then whispered "Arghh! It hurts so Freaking bad!!!!"

Then Osirus Punched Ernest And tugged On him, causing Both Of them to roll at high Speed In that Condition, Ernest Threw Osirus Hard Causing the two to separate and Osirus to fall hard on the ground meanwhile Ernest got Bumped Because of the throw and a stretch in his left leg.

Then Ernest, with the pain in his leg stood at rest meanwhile, Osirus was holding his forehead that got hurt.

Then As Osirus Was standing slowly, Maintaining Balance Ernest came sprinting and from the back of Osirus, he held his neck and tried choking him.

"w-wwaaa..hat ohhh!!! Ahhhh!" Osirus gagged.

Then Osirus tried vigorously to remove Ernest's strong hands, catching hold of his neck.

But, nothing happened.

Osirus, who struggled in the clutches Of Ernest's hands Tried Removing the hands and moved them a bit giving him some breathing space, then Pushed Ernest. Causing Him to get free of the hold Then he Stood, Stretching his hands, satisfying each nerve in his arms.

Before Ernest Could Stand back And Dominate Osirus, Osirus himself Kicked Him in the face Causing him to fall.

As Osirus Launched his leg on Ernest's face It was stopped by him, Ernest caught hold of the Leg and threw him a few metres away. Then Stood Ernest Slowly. Osirus rushed to punch Ernest, But he dodged that and launched a Punch on Osirus making him fall on the ground on his face.

Then Ernest, trying to look cool laid down on the body of Osirus, resting.

Osirus tried standing up only for him to realize that Ernest had laid flat on him. Taking a view at the sky. Osirus Tried a lot of force but his bad, He couldn't get up, then he just shook his own body on his left side like an absolute dog and sloped it causing Ernest to fall hard even though he fell at a low height.

Then Osirus Stood up on his knees and started Punching Ernest on his face. He punched Ernest 34 times and, causing Ernest's eye to be sore.

Then Ernest kicked Osirus's face who had his tongue out drooling, causing Osirus to react to the trash taste of the shoe.

"Ahh! Eww It's gross ." Said Osirus in disgust.

"Hah! Got ya Brotha."

Then Before Ernest Could Launch a punch, when Osirus was disturbed by the taste of the shoes that came on his tongue.

Came Ernest's punch on Osirus's face, but fortunate for him, he was able to change the direction of the punch. After he did it, he stood instantaneously and kicked Ernest on his butt, causing him to lose balance and fall to the ground on his face.

Then Ernest Stood Only to get wwelcomed with Osirus's punch and fall on the ground again. Then Osirus kicked him straight up on his face. Then stood up swiftly, collapsed Ernest kicked Osirus on his chest. Causing him to collapse on the ground 2 meters away. Osirus then stood as he could, only to get hit in the stomach with punches consecutively 8 times, him dripping Saliva.

Finally, After all the Painful punches, Came the kick of Ernest on his face. Fortunately enough, Osirus didn't stick out his tongue. His taste buds were fine. But he did get hurt on his face and you can even make out that he fought with someone and got himself beaten by just looking at his face. In simple words, he looked like he had mud thrown on him and he spread it on his face like a 2-year-old.

They Both continued Fighting each other.

On the contrary, Shaun was busy repairing his broken car. The car could now move at the speed of 30 Kilometers and run for around 10 hours. That's pretty fine, the only thing is that. At this speed, they'll take more than weeks to even reach Kashmir. So, he has decided that he'll try driving the car, without any safety ropes attached. Even though he won't drive without these measures. But who would like to waste energy and effort, when you can just do smart work?

So Shaun Jumped In the car. Turned it on and tried driving it. The first five minutes went like a driving test. Slow, tense, fear of the unknown, and lastly '*Monotonous*'.

But just right after the Five minutes were over. The car started slowing down and became questionable. Will it even drive further more? Or will it break down?

Well, the car started performing better and became normal. But again, it was damn slow and Monotonous!

Meanwhile, Javon, who had made deadly progress on opening a box was still opening the box, whereas the other seven Assassins were controlling the army and preparing for any potential attacks.

While he was opening the box, taking Time. Came one of his army's Fellow assassins and this guy asks "Leader! I wondered if you are Opening the box, that consists of powers right ?"

"Yes, are you not aware or what."

"S...so I had to ask, can I get some of the parts of the box's powers ?" He asked.

"Have you done anything, huh? What Shit have you contributed towards us huh!" Said Javon in a toxic tone.

Now anyone seeing that Idiot Assassin can make out that he's controlling his bladder out from peeing, as he was intimidated.

But still, he said "W....Well... I-I 've broken down one whole Pillar at that p-p-pla-ce."

Then stopped Javon his work and said Sarcastically in a Low tone "Noice! Well then come and kneel here."

That Guy lost all his guts to say shit and just kneeled.

Then Javon took a Katana in his hands and swung it hard and Slit!! That assassin was dead, him beheaded, no head on his body and the head fell Distant.

Then Javon whispered to himself "Bastard."

Meanwhile, Osirus and Ernest, Hit each other For 2 hours with both of them looking like they carried out labour at a construction site. At least for now, the both of them were lying on the grass, injured and tired. Both of them contemplated the fight.

Ernest who was impressed with Osirus's stronghold in Combat and grasping power, was himself Injured badly by a literal Beginner.

Then Said Ernest exhausted "I am sleeping on this grass."

"(Sigh) Me too!."

And went Five minutes, where Ernest Fell Asleep, meanwhile Osirus staring at the sky as if he was dead and attained eternal happiness in the afterlife.

Then, Came the speeding car of Shaun, which had somehow caught up to the speed of 50Kmph. I mean pretty decent for a trash car, the only thing's that it's gonna stop working fast.

The car was coming in the path where Ernest, who was asleep, and Osirus looking in the blue were.

The dozing Ernest woke up in shock after hearing the loud noise from the car and so did Osirus.

They both stood, looking at the dust-covered car, with a few visible dents and cracks on the car. Especially the headlights, Broken, Looking like a battery which is been used on a science project, Messy. The Car was working but the fastest it could go is around 70Kmph. Which is well decent but not that fast, because they have to commit well.. a whole frickin genocide for that Crap Box.

"How fast will it go?" Asked Ernest.

"70Kmph probably." said Shaun

"Isn't it too slow?" Said Ernest.

"Yeah Dawg, I have to work a bit to get some 30Kmph extra speed."

"How long will it take for you to fix the car so much?" Questioned Osirus.

"Probably 4 hours."

"Well sounds okay, but better finish it by today or else we are going to be done for." Said Ernest.

"(yawn) Yeah I'll try."

Then went inside the super sleep-deprived Shaun, Who looked like he had insomnia. He continued driving the car away from the ground and took it to his repair spot.

Ernest Checked the time and it was 5 AM.

"What the hell !!, we've been fighting for so damn long!" Said Ernest "So fighting with Osirus is pretty...... *interesting*".

Osirus said, "Do you want me to shove my leg into you?"

"Why what happened ?"

"You don't know ?? Aren't we fighting!" said Osirus

"Ohh!! Nah we ain't fighting, let me take some darn rest, I am already pretty tired fighting you, and anyways after 2 hours I am gonna have a final training with ya." Said Ernest.

"Yeah, it's gonna be so frickin easy beating you to a pulp." Said Osirus.

"Hell naw Dawg, I ain't holding back on my powers this time, I am gonna use my powers on you."

"What the hell dude! you didn't teach me to use my magic." Said Osirus In shock.

"I ain't the person who's gonna teach ya magic, I don't even know how your magic works, cuz your Magic works differently."

"You better be foolin' around Ernest." conveyed Osirus "If you're being real, then I am frickin not coming with you!"

"Well.... I am not kidding around, I am being Honest, I am gonna use my powers, and anyway, not every time you are gonna have the advantage, you will have to face such bad conditions and you gotta accept this and fight." Said Ernest "You are not gonna be at the advantage everytime, there's a reason why the box is with the Assassins and not with us!"

"What the hell dude, how in the world am I gonna smack you a punch in such a condition??" Asked Osirus.

"By using your magical powers against me, You ain't Batman to just jerk around without having powers, you have powers. Use 'em and use your upper floor, you'll get it."

As soon as Ernest Said that crap, he left walking away from there.

In Osirus's mind *How tf can I defeat him and do some Shit damage to him?, He's definitely joking around, or maybe not* was going on and kept on contemplating about what he had heard.

Meanwhile, on Creed's base. The security had jerked up. The Assassins were placed almost everywhere on the tall mountain. Sirius was busy making a strong gun. With some assassins along with a strong Rocket Launcher. While all these measures were happening. Javon was busy opening the box. He had opened up about 25,985 layers of the box of the 30,000 layers.

He had been there for a heck long time. Anyone can recognize it by seeing his clothes, Mushy and sweaty. He had his hands extremely numbed and after removing these many layers of the box all that was left were a few thousand more layers of protection on the box. The box had become significantly slender.

Finally, Javon gave his hands some rest and removed his sweat-sleek dress, releasing a high amount of sweat as if it were a small waterfall. Then walked down Javon, throwing Sleek close to the box, and went downstairs to the base. He was faced with fellow Assassins training under Sangorath. As he walked up, all the Assassins Looked up at Javon, their leader with his Shredded muscular body, smooth hair, and a little bit of beard on his jaw.

Then he asked Sangorath "What've they achieved ?"

"Some kinda progress like Better combat, Experience in Spears, Katanas, and Kunais." Said Sangorath.

"Good! now continue what you're doing, no rest time for your arse." Said Javon in satisfaction.

Then Javon Continued towards Sirius at his arsenal, where he was making Weapons along with some Assassins.

He walked in to find the arsenal with an enormous amount of weapons.

"How are ya gonna distribute these many big amounts of weapons?" Asked Javon.

"Don't worry about that."

"(Sigh) Fine.." Said Javon low toned and walked away.

Meanwhile, Shaun had significantly fixed the Car, with the car having the glass fixed so it's difficult to recognize the bullet hits and the headlights had become nice like new, and well... the car can finally move at a speed of 120Kmph.

But the doors were bent at places, which ain't a big deal as it's repaired for reaching certain places, not for some kinda show-off.

Meanwhile, Osirus who was contemplating almost for an hour about what he should

do finally stopped contemplating and came up with a counter to the magical power attacks

of Ernest, who was resting on a hammock. Osirus, who is intimidated as if Ernest is gonna murder him and eat him.

Shaun did a driving test on his fixed car where finally the car could feel fast and smooth and so he continued driving it and decided to drift it and noticed that it was getting loose while drifting and slipping at times due to lack of friction.

But it wasn't a big deal and the car caught speed in no time and began to go fast and in front, Shaun could see a wooden pole.

He said, "Hell naw I have to drift this car."

As he tried drifting, the tires got slippery.

"Holy Shit!, brakes !"

He shouted all that he could and fortunately, just close to the pole, he stopped and said "I ain't trying drifting again."

On the other side, Ernest who was in a deep nap, woke up, well-rested and energized to train Osirus.

Meanwhile, Osirus was terrified as hell but finally convinced himself to be brave and jumped twice to stimulate himself.

Ernest, who woke up from his nap gargled his mouth with water and washed his face, and finally got himself tightened up to cross hands with Osirus.

CHAPTER SEVEN

Osirus was terrified about what he had to deal with. It is an unfair fighting exam, which will be Embarrassing for him to lose if he messes up a lot. Ernest was walking all the way tight whereas Osirus was constantly overthinking about the worst scenarios that could happen in the battle. Will he get Smashed? Will he die and look like a metamorphic rock? Will he be able to eat anything? Is it worth Fighting and getting injured? All of these kinds of questions were popping up inside Osirus's Terrified Mind.

Finally, Osirus decided to have the guts to face it, give his all out, and walk with all the courage he could make up towards Ernest.

As soon as Osirus was closing his fists tight to get them prepared said Ernest "Bro, Don't tryna be dominative when you know you are messed up, at least don't lie, dang!"

"Heh (giggles) I ain't going easy on ya."

"Sounds like some scared kid would say this." Said Ernest. "c'mon you don't have to be that terrified about this."

"R..really ?" asked Osirus.

"Yeah." Said Ernest.

"You Gonna be at ease?"

"Nah." Said Ernest "but not on a murder level."

"Oh !" Said Osirus.

Osirus had now tightened his fists up to strike Ernest, but before he could, an icy, crystal solid blue Hard Spike of the Magic of Ernest, struck Straight in Osirus's Chest, throwing him 3 metres far hard on the ground. Osirus even before he stood on his legs, was welcomed by Another Strong spike Wave coming towards him at the sound speed which hit and broke into small particles sending him to the ground and Bleeding out his lips.

Ernest was swiftly Running towards Osirus and his blue Magical powers joined from the grass roots.

"Holy cow!" Said Osirus "How am I supposed to throw these things up?"

Osirus Sprinted and sent a punch flowing on Ernest, but Ernest Caught hold of the Hand and walloped the fluid Powers straight into Osirus's solar plexus, resulting in a mild slit. With A thin flow of blood dripping from the plexus, Osirus was falling to the ground Losing consciousness. But fortunately, the slit was getting compact, yet it was smarting at the slit getting compact.

"Bro use your magic, you ain't Batman!" Said Ernest in frustration.

Osirus Stood and thought about how to eject The Magical Powers.

Before he could realise anything, Ernest struck him with a strong punch. Ernest was about to launch another punch at him, sending him collapsing to the ground. But, as the punch was about to hit, came Osirus's strong punch Which had the magenta-shaded Fluid along. throwing a strong strike on Ernest. Sending him a bit up only to collapse the grass.

"(Grunting) Finally!" said Osirus "But what the hell did I do? And was it right?"

"Ahhh! (Sigh) stop with your anxiety, It's freaking annoying!" Said Ernest in annoyance.

He swiftly stood with blue wobbly looking powers and threw it in meteoric speed towards Osirus, which blew up on Osirus's face. Causing him to throw up blood from his throat. With him injured and feeling like his throat was slit, all he could feel was he had slit in the throat, more like a burning sensation from Black pepper overdose.

Osirus's eyes, popped with red nerves, leaving him looking like he was about to die holding his throat, it left an opportunity for Ernest to launch another power attack, but he just ran and kicked Osirus, straight in the centre of his chest, leaving him collapsed on the grass. Well, Ernest showed generosity by doin' that, that's what it tells.

"Bro, I didn't slit your throat, it's just you overcomplicating shit." Said Ernest "There's a reason why you feel the pain in all the encounters with those Assassins and pretty much the first one to be taken down, just.....learn to embrace pain and endure it!"

Hearing, came a kick From Osirus, which Landed directly on Ernest's left knee joint, resulting in him collapsing on the ground as if his leg was sniped.

"oww.... (panting) Yeah you gettin' there." Said Ernest.

Osirus launched a kick straight at Ernest's mouth and tried pushing it inside his mouth to make karma equal. Ernest could feel the pressure, despite being stronger than Osirus, he could barely speak anything. He felt like at any moment, his gums might bleed. Moving through his oesophagus, slitting the throat muscles and going into the stomach with all the blood, only to be burned by gastric acid.

But to reduce that possibility, Ernest tried holding his hands on the dirt-scarred sneakers of Osirus and fortunate for him, he managed to throw the shoe from his mouth, leaving behind linger and disgusting taste on his tongue.

"eh (cough) what the hell!" Said Ernest, disgust on his face and a smirk from filth "Where the hell do you get these ideas ?!"

"Moron, you've done this shit to me as well, as

> *"*"Even if you go to Burma, you can never escape Karma"*"*

is said for a frickin' reason." Said Osirus.

"Who are you, a philosopher? And who said this?" Asked Ernest.

"Your Uncle" replied Osirus.

"Dawg!" Said Ernest "(giggles) At least I have a philosopher uncle, unlike you!"

"You damn idi-" said Osirus.

He was smacked stiff with Ernest's fist, which looked like it was poisoned blue. When it hit Osirus's face, it created the sound of sharp ice breaking. The sound of the powers that Ernest used.

Osirus had some severe injuries on his face. One huge slit, between the left side of his nose and his left eye's sclera.

Osirus now had cuts similar to the ones caused by glass.

"Ah, shit." Said Osirus in extreme affliction.

"Oh shit!" said Ernest "Just frickin heal it."

"You idiot piece of crap can't ya see, I am in literal pain, l-i-t-e-r-a-l! (groan)" Said Osirus furiously.

Ernest was unable to utter anything, he was left speechless.

"(groaning........) Bro!! Hey! Help me, why are you death staring at me, the pain is increasing!??"

"It's healing blind idiot." Said Ernest "That's why it's stinging".

"Oh."

"Now I am unlocking another slit on your face!" Said Ernest.

"Ayo what!"

The strong Ice-clear sharp magical glacier came straight at Osirus in Swiftness. It was about to hit Osirus, but he Jerked to the left side in extreme swiftness, faster than a mosquito and before Ernest could react to that, he could feel a strong Kick impact on his butt. Which sent his Butt in shock and His spinal cord for seconds. He could not sense anything. Only he jerked up to see Osirus on the side, who sided from getting hit by his punch has swiftly cocked his leg Towards Ernest's butt to make him collapse.

"What the hell is this" Whispered Ernest.

He wondered how in the world Osirus managed to do that because, for others, he acts like an absolute monkey.

"You Getting there, my (giggles) guy" Said Ernest.

"Thanks." Appreciated Osirus.

"Um, Now take this Homie!" Said Ernest.

"What the-" said Osirus in surprise.

He was blootered by Ernest on his face. Agonizing Osirus.

Before he could even stand on his knees, he was booted from Ernest.

Osirus had a thin flow of blood from his nose.

Osirus groaned in exhaustion, stinging, irritation and burning sensation. He felt like he had VapoRub on his philtrum, resulting in burning sensations in his nostrils.

"Shit" Groaned Osirus.

Ernest on the other hand was feeling tired, fighting Osirus.

"(giggles) You (spits saliva down the ground) exhausting the shit out of me now".

"Well, sounds nice to me." Replied Osirus.

They both use their throat voice box to extreme loudness and dart towards each other with a closed and strong fist to break Jaws.

As Osirus approached, he took his first to hit it on Ernest. It flew and punched straight on Ernest's lip, rigid. With the lip slit open, came blood flowing down. Ernest has blood spat out his mouth and a slit on his lip.

As Ernest processed what he just faced he spoke "Aghhh..... (giggles), not bad brotha."

Osirus just stared straight into Ernest's eyes, dead still with no reaction on his face.

Ernest Struck his left hand straight into Osirus's abdomen. Spreading shockwaves around. His staring was interrupted.

Ernest had prepared himself and jerked up an icy magical fluid stroke on Osirus but before he could strike it on him. Osirus cocked up a heavy Punch straight in Ernest's chest, sending his ribs vibrating and thrown distant on the ground. Ernest collapsed hard on the ground, his head struck hard on the grassy ground, and he was hit by a rock. Which commenced a lake of blood from his crown. The blood moved and bathed the grass beneath his body.

"uggghhhh!!! (Gasps) Nice one." Said Ernest "You've progressed a heck of a lot."

"Thanks, Bro." Said Osirus.

"Just make sure to use that shit, your brain."

"Wait that's....... Freaky suspicious???"

"Ye Coward you got it right!" Exclaimed Ernest.

Before Osirus could respond anything, he was struck with a strong Kick, that landed straight on his Schlong.

He experienced extreme pain, his nerves spiking. Osirus was pushed with a lot of force by that kick and it ended with him collapsing on the ground, in excruciating and unbearable pain.

"Arghhhh!! (Groaning) Crap!" agonized Osirus.

"Stupid, you gonna be trapped like this anytime and you gonna believe whatever someone spits out?" Said Ernest "(stood up) Idiot just shut up and beat the crap out of your opponent!"

"(groan) Okay." Replied Osirus.

Ernest kicked Osirus again down there, increasing the pain.

"I said Shut up- ugh."

Ernest was kicked straight on his jaw by agonized Osirus's right leg's sneaker heel, who wasn't doing well with the agony, especially with being hit in the same area again.

Osirus had a weird spiky pain in his nerves.

Ernest got a rip in the skin of his jaw, resulting in bleeding. The blood is shaped like a piece of Potato peel with the blood apple-red.

The rip created a stingy sensation at the skin tear.

The ripped skin had fallen half, with one half on Osirus's sneaker's dirty midsole.

"Hah! (Groan) I teared up a portion of your skin" Exclaimed Osirus "But looks gross."

The ripped piece of skin looked like a tiny thin cut of tomato, translucent.

After Osirus spoke out his words, as he was 'bout to stand, he was struck with the blue as smooth as microalgae fluid-like Blow from Ernest targeted in his Solar plexus. Sending him to a backflip, only to strike stiffly on the natural grass in his mouth. His Jaw had huge waves of vibration in it, but lucky for him, no bad linger.

Osirus, whose spine felt doozy, his jaw shaky, could barely stand plumb. He could not even stand as askew as a Homo habile.

As Osirus attempted to stand erect, he was Cocked up with a stiff hammer hit, from Ernest from his left hand, holding the fist tight for the blue opaque hammer.

Osirus was sent stuff on the ground. A thin river fall of Blood started flowing from Osirus's left side of the mouth. The blood along with saliva drooled on the grass, bathing it. The grass around the opening of blood was all patterned and tattooed in blood-like designs. Osirus's cuspid was bleeding from a thin yet deep slit resulting from friction, resulting in a deep cut. Due to the strike, the teeth around the cuspid broke free out of the gum area, and the mouth was covered in a waxy layer of blood, as red as a Tomato.

"Ah Shit, I guess I murdered him." Said, Ernest.

As Ernest approached further, he felt more intimidated, did he just commit a homicide? He wondered.

"Ahh crap." said Ernest terrified "Is he frickin dead?"

Ernest, who finished approaching the closest to Osirus, thought he messed up badly. But, only shortly after, he sensed life going on. Heart pumping, blood flowing, brain working, immune system running up. And all that he could sense was a conscious, alive and strong Osirus with pain, but before he could respond to the knowledge.

A strong boot came straight at his schlong.

His thousands of Nerves, which absorbed the shock from the kick were all skewered. His eyes widened, the nerves popping clear. Ernest Collapsed in extreme agony on the grassy ground, with another shock from the back from the tiny pebbles in the green grass.

It was Osirus who kicked Ernest straight with a donned sneaker in the right leg.

He was erect with blood in his mouth like he had his whole gum full of cuts from broken pieces of glass.

Osirus holding his jaw In pain gagged "Ughh! crap, You are a freak dude, A freak!"

"(groaning) piece of crap! Ughh!" Snapped Ernest. "Now I have a shit ton of trust issues with ya (groans)"

"Well, doesn't matter to me." Muttered Osirus.

Landing another strong kick straight on Ernest's chest.

The kick in the chest sent Ernest breathless. He realised that Osirus acts like an absolute scared cat. But, wild as hell.

"Bro, You frickin broke my teeth." Spoke Osirus with his broken teeth "pretty much the whole down front row."

"Idiot, they haven't come out, have they?"

"They are falling" Gagged Osirus.

Osirus spat the broken teeth out. The broken blood covered teeth, as they fell hard blood dried on them, like wax coating.

Osirus looked like he was kicked to shit by a bunch of street goons with a crowbar.

As Ernest tried to Erect, he was jerked with a kick in the face from Osirus. Which sent Ernest, down to the ground.

As Osirus Kicked groaned Ernest in Pain.

At last, Osirus drew his hand straight at Ernest's neck, held it firm and pulled him up.

Ernest Stood with all the injuries.

"You are wild as shit." Said Ernest "But still not satisfied-."

Osirus caught hold of him, brought him to his knees and strangled Ernest as strongly as he could. Ernest Gagged hard before Osirus threw him fast on the ground. Ernest, who collapsed straight on the ground, had a lot of stones that hit him. He noticed various cramps in his whole body.

Osirus was all Injured, his nose was dried out with burns, and his mouth had blood dried with a thin flow. His Gums bled out terribly. His back was all in pain from shock absorption.

As Osirus walked towards Ernest, he felt dizzy and collapsed on the ground with all the cuts and injuries.

They both gasped as the fight got over.

"(sigh) Do teeth grow, because of Healing?" Asked Osirus.

"I donno my guy (gasps)." Said Ernest.

"You haven't tried?"

"Bro, my teeth are strong, unlike your Milk teeth of a baby!"

"So, I am going for surgery now to a dentist to get fake teeth."

"Idiot, you going now for what?" Asked Ernest "Seriously, now at this moment for what reason?"

"Cause, we fighting those Assassins." Answered Osirus.

"How in the world are teeth gonna help you fight them!?" Asked Ernest "Are you high or what, are they gonna simp you for your teeth and die of that? Huh? Of course frickin not."

"But I want to!"

"Shut your mouth up, you ain't going for a fashion to fight 'em and they probably might get healed."

"(relief)"

"Only if it's not that severe."

"Ah! No!" yelled Osirus.

"Sucks to suck." Said Ernest.

As Osirus contemplated his lost teeth Ernest recovered from the wounds. Came Shaun driving the car.

It came all in Swift, looking great and decent. The headlights seemed great, but the white colour became kinda dull. But, the car seemed great.

The electric car could finally run without any problems, it looked fine except for a few bullet hits.

"Howdy............" Said, Shaun.

Only to see both of them on the ground.

"Don't tell me, you both just fought like mad street dogs?" Questioned Shaun.

"(Sigh) Yeah." Answered Ernest.

"Okay, but why do you seem like you are beaten to shit by a bunch of people?"

"Cause I beat the shit out of him and cracked his -"

"You cracked his what!" Snapped Shaun.

"Don't ask." Said Osirus.

"Bro Ernest, you lost." Said Shaun "To this Kid, are you kidding me?"

"No basically umm.... Yeah I lost, but I did break his teeth."

"But I did kick you in your-"

"Don't talk about it, I can do that shit as well."

"Ahh! Never mind, my braincells are not braincelling now, just.... Shut up." Said, Shaun.

"Btw, the car is fixed and can run at around 160 Kmph. So we can finally reach fast now."

"But doesn't it slip while drifting?" Asked Ernest.

"Wait, How do you know that shit?"

"Cause I had just woken up at that time when you were doing that Arse test."

"Oh!, never mind." Said Shaun "But, how are you gonna come in this condition to fight there?"

"I will recover by then." Replied Ernest.

"I know, I am asking about this other fish lying down."

"Who knows." Said Ernest "He barely has any teeth in the down row and speaks like you with a broken Jaw, I mean similarly."

"Won't he recover?"

"Probably." Said Ernest.

"Will the teeth recover?" Asked Osirus.

"Yes, they can," said Shaun.

"Hush." Relieved Osirus.

"But hardly possible."

"Arghh!"

"Never mind, let's have lunch."

"Wait, what's that? We didn't have it yesterday?" Asked Osirus.

"Cause you didn't even have breakfast." Said Shaun "At least now eat Lunch."

"(Sigh) fine."

"What's there tho for lunch?" Asked Ernest.

"Some rice." Said, Shaun.

"And what else."

"Only Rice"

"Weird". Said Ernest "(sigh) Fine let's go."

"What about me?" Asked Osirus "I can't eat rice with these teeth."

"Then don't eat". Said Ernest.

"Arghhh!"

"(sigh) let's go." Said Shaun "We don't have all day."

"(sigh) fine." Said Ernest.

The three went to their shelter, a Blue pyramid tent beside which were two thick erect wooden sticks for Ernest to sleep and put on his hammock.

Meanwhile, Osirus slept in the tent.

Ernest and Shaun, had water with them, to make the rice in a plastic Container. Both of 'em placed the warm water from a small electric water heater cup. The rice became soft and mushy. The white rice had slowly begun to cook, which released a great amount of smoke, which was a delight in a cold mountain."

Whereas Osirus was cleansing his blood-painted mouth with salty water.

As Shaun and Ernest placed the lid back on the box, the smoke got trapped and the rice. Began steaming hot.

"(relief) finally rice." Said Ernest "But would've been better if it was biryani."

"The container Biryanis from supermarkets or grocery stores are shit, taste artificial and don't have that citric, spicy, addictive and flavourful taste." Said, Shaun.

"So it basically would be shit that we would eat." Said Ernest.

"Exactly."

The two took a steel spoon out and took a delightful bite out of the soft wet white rice.

As it touched their mouth with the spoon, they were in delight at the rice.

"pretty decent." Said Ernest "But, could've been better with a soft-boiled Egg or a sunny side up."

"No eggs with me." Said, Shaun.

"I know My guy, That's why I said *Could've been*."

Meanwhile, Osirus sat his butt down on a mattress on the ground. Seeing Shaun and Ernest eating a proper Lunch, meanwhile him, eating a ripe yellow banana. He ate the banana with his gums and wisdom teeth.

As he chewed the banana, he felt pain. He could feel his gums stinging.

As he consumed the banana, he kept staring like a person with insomnia. His eyes were completely staring at the satisfaction of his friends eating rice. Around his eyes, his skin had turned pink due to the punches rubbing the skin, producing the damn friction.

As he kept staring at 'em, he eventually finished the banana. In his mind, he wondered how in the world magic could not recover his teeth.

The powers can fix a broken bone, save its user or a person from dying due to stabbing or being shot, save from various medical conditions and probably even revive a body part that is amputated. But not a frickin layer of teeth.

As he realised that his banana was over, he kept the peel in a good place and just stared at Ernest and Shaun devouring their rice.

"Do you guys ever get Hypothermia?" questioned Osirus.

"Nah." Said Shaun "We have an immune system way ahead of others, cuz of the powers and Hypothermia is a thing which you can get, not us."

"I am not feeling cold though." Said Osirus.

"Cuz this ain't a proper hill station and there are factories over here." Said Ernest.

"Yeah, asking 'bout Hypothermia is like asking if I eat something healthy and fresh, will I get diarrhoea." Said, Shaun.

"(sigh) Fine shut up now." Said Osirus.

Afterwards, he just didn't say anything. He took another banana and devoured it with his remaining 26 teeth.

As he finished eating the banana, Shaun and Ernest also finished their rice bowl and went to the car and prepare. Whereas Osirus, Sat and contemplated all that he learnt and did.

On the other hand, Ernest and Shaun had Their glocks loaded with 20 bullets in the magazine and had additional bullets and magazines.

They packed all the things and bags in the car itself.

As Osirus sat on the mattress, Ernest came in.

"Hey! Come now, we have to go now." Said Ernest.

Osirus said "(sigh) k."

Osirus stood up took his bag and packed up everything required. As they left, there was no hammock, no wooden support for one, and no tents, the place was all empty with a few areas with blood and the broken teeth of Osirus.

As Osirus was about to sit in the car, he saw The blood-dried fountain pen, below the seat. He was surprised that it didn't get lost.

"Woah! This thing is still there." wondered Osirus.

"Bro get ya butt in the frickin car." Said Ernest.

"Yeah."

Osirus took his legs donned with sneakers straight in the car.

As he entered, he bent and his hips finally rested on the car.

Osirus rested on the car seat with Ernest and closed the door hard. Leading shake In the car.

"Oh, this trembling is suspicious!" Said Osirus.

As Osirus stayed in the car with all that of cold. He realised that his clothes were smelling bad and pretty mushy.

"Ah! Shit, these clothes (sigh) smell like shit." Said Osirus.

Osirus believed that they were going to fight anyway and it's gonna get dirty there so he could just change after the battle. But the concerning factor was his jeans, extremely uncomfortable to don. He decided to change it as it was getting annoying and could probably irritate him and probably even cause a rash. He ended up changing the jeans while Shaun and Ernest warmed up for battle.

Osirus removed his bag and brought out His Navy Blue trousers to don. As he exchanged the jeans with trousers, he could immediately feel the difference. He could feel the Ecstasy and Solace. He didn't give a crap now. As he stared at his friends with the sun behind slowly going over. Contemplating all that he confronted all this time.

As he kept wondering. He abruptly felt the electric energy passing and powering the car. It was Shaun who finished the warmup with Ernest. Everyone had sat inside the car and the car slowly commenced towards the exit as the car went speeding down the road on the mountain. The car moved with high speed with Ernest and Shaun in dead silence and blear.

The car went almost as smoothly as a new one. The car sped down 185 kilometres per hour on the road. The car went in different turns that no one ever went.

"Where is that shitty base?" Asked Osirus.

"At the end boundaries of Himachal Pradesh." Replied Shaun.

"What the hell!" Exclaimed Osirus "We will take heck a lot of time reachin' there."

"We are literally at the end of Haryana." Said Ernest.

"But still."

"We are going fast and if you don't know the car is frickin going at 230 KMPH." Said, Shaun.

"Wait wtf." Said Osirus.

"We're already in between of Punjab." Said Ernest.

"Wtf."

"We are taking roots you are not aware," said Ernest "No one frickin knows these routes, cause well they aren't seen."

"So how long will it take to reach to them?"

"2 hours, 30 minutes, 37 seconds, 69 milliseconds, 55 microseconds, 16,567,230 nanoseconds and-"

"Ayo What the hell Shaun, why making up shit." Said Osirus "Is it real."

"I mean the hours and minutes are real and the other shit……. Well…." Said, Shaun.

"(Sigh) Continue." Said Osirus.

As they continued, Osirus could feel that the car was getting faster and could barely feel electricity passing the car for a Femtosecond.

As he comprehended, the car had already reached the end of Punjab. As a few 200 metres away to cross the state to reach Himachal Pradesh.

"What the hell is going on???" Asked Osirus.

"We've reached pretty close." Said Ernest.

"Suckers, if you could do this, why the hell didn't you guys do that before?" Questioned Osirus.

"Of course not Dumbo." Said Shaun "We'll take time to reach."

"Round how much?" Asked Osirus.

"(sigh) We'll take 4 hours to reach there." Said, Shaun.

"Isn't it like 2 PM already?"

"It's 1 PM." Said Ernest.

"Not that if he knew."

"So all those things you yapped were fake?" Said Osirus.

"Yeah." Said Shaun "I m-mean not everything, like the secret routes do frickin exist and we are going through one right now if you are not aware."

"(sigh) fine."

As the car approached forward, the quieter it became outside. All that was visible were roughs and terrains and a taupe-brown turf route. With the sun reflecting rays on the car hot.

As the car moved further, the wheels with bumps on the taupe brown turf, capering with shallow bumps. Osirus's leaning head bumped up the window as he was silent.

2 hours passed with the three silent as a mute. Contemplating all they could.

"How long away are we to get me beaten up?" Asked Osirus.

"Don't ask me questions Osirus!" Said Shaun "You can frickin see me cocking up to this steering wheel without saying anything!"

"Wait listen just–"

"Shut up!" Said, Shaun.

"Dawgs, stop fighting."

"Do your own thing and shut up." Said, Shaun.

"Geez" Whispered Osirus.

"And Osirus, we are currently in Pathankot, Punjab." Said Ernest.

"Okay' sighed Osirus "But where in the world is Pathankot!"

"You know Geography Dawg?" Asked Ernest "I mean have you ever looked up for G.K. We had frickin Geographical questions the whole darn school life."

"I never got such questions, I mean I messed them to shit I guess."

"And the fact that you are broke as shit." Said Shaun "I mean, you are a Freaking freelancer, you are broke AF. I mean c'mon, can only earn ?10,000 a project. Like how many tons of projects have you got, as much as cow dung."

"Don't go on the pay." Said Osirus "I have a frickin bungalow!"

"So what, I also have one, Ernest owns one. I mean 10,000. If I sell my fingernail. It will still be more valuable than ?10,000."

"At least I am earning."

"I am earning too, And I earn 500 times more than what you earn." Said, Shaun.

"Stop fighting Idiots!" Said Ernest.

Osirus sighed with frustration and chugged down water from his stiff glass 3-litre bottle.

The car abided even as further it could get.

As they argued, they had crossed the states of Punjab, entering the cold Mistful and full of bliss and minute white particles descending.

The turns of the routes were overlong which if driven properly, would result in smoothness. As the car approached the turn, the smoother it felt like driving on an icy road.

As the car proceeded further. The more the white snowy particles Glimpsed transparent.

And finally, after more than 2 hours and 30 minutes, the car reached, the sight of a mountain ginormous. Sheltered with trees.

"Is it where we are supposed to be?" Asked Osirus.

"Yeah." Said Ernest.

"So what now?"

"What? What the hell do you mean what?? we have to massacre 'em." Said, Shaun.

"(Sigh) Bro! Go frickin easy." said Ernest.

"The hell is your deal dude?" snapped Osirus.

"Arghhhh!, shut your frickin mouths both of ya!" Snapped Ernest "I'll fricking shoot both of you in your toxic-ass brains!."

"(sigh) fine." They both voiced.

As they resolved the conflict, they could feel some kind of energy, like a border, penetrated. As they approached, they felt a heavy bump up the car only till it had penetrated.

Only after a minute or two of the car penetrated. It launched off the steep slope of the mountain, which was a route to the base. As the car geared up the slope on the road. They could see a blood-red ribbionish swing coming to the car. It was Jules, the first Assassin. He came in a swift swim from the air straight at the front of the car. Stiff in his arm was a dagger, with a grey blade and, black handle with orange scales.

"Who the hell is that!" snapped Shaun.

"Atlantas? Sangorath?"

"I believe it's J-Juliet." Said Osirus.

"You mean that Jules?" questioned Ernest.

"Probably-."

"Rascals, he's coming straight at us!" shouted Shaun.

"Oh, crap." The three spoke together.

Before they could respond to Jules, he landed straight up on the car's bonnet.

"Shit." Said Osirus.

"Shut up!" said Shaun. "Ernest, what's cookin'?"

No reply from Ernest, only after a moment for him to draw his Glock pistol out to shoot, to thrust the glass, to pierce it through and before he could do. All he realised was that would've Messed up the situation, then already it had become. As he realised, he peeked his head up to the torso. As Ernest jerked the gun aiming straight at Jules's frontal skull. As Jules noticed, he jerked his dagger straight at the barrel. The dagger swung straight cutting the gun barrel smooth.

"Oh crap." Snapped Ernest.

As half a barrel fell off behind, Ernest was doomed.

As Jules swung the Dagger straight into Ernest's chest. As it reached, he jerked up his hand. Cocking up the dagger. A slit was incepted with blood moving fast out. As Jules pushed the dagger with more force. The more blood came out.

Ernest Snapped with an ache. As his palm bled.

Ernest could feel his nerves in pressure, his arteries slit. As he could not hold the dagger more tight. It began slipping from the palms. Approaching towards the heart, to stab it. Jules became impatient and as he was about to speed up went behind Ernest and stabbed him. His jaw was smashed straight from the left kick Shaun booted on. Sending Jules off the path and behind the car, collapsed on the ground.

As Jules was gone, Ernest could relieve with the huge slit on his left palm.

"Arghh! My hand's skewered." Groaned Ernest.

"Ernest!, You well?" Asked Osirus.

"Yeah, I am fine." Sighed Ernest.

"Osirus, take out some bandages!" Snapped Shaun in panic.

"Pay your damn attention at driving, Shaun!" Yelled Ernest, groaning.

Osirus Jerked up his backpack and grabbed up the bandage roll.

"Take!" Said Osirus.

As Ernest snatched the roll in pain.

"But stop the bleeding?" Questioned Osirus.

"I don't need to." Said Ernest in almost minimal to no voice "My bleeding will get patched, it's just there for protection."

"(sigh) You Idiot as hell for a reason." Said Osirus.

"Shut up!" Ranted Shaun.

Ernest who had the 3 metres width wide bandage roll, donned straight at his arm. As he wrapped It around the palm. Leaving only the fingers open.

As the car went further. They could see a stone-textured, wall-shaped Oblong. In the centre was a wooden door. Coloured Teak Brown.

It was just 55 metres away. As the car speeds up. Came another Assassin, with the red ribbon-shaped bloody Magic lingering behind. Peeked at it, it was Atlantas, the second Assassin. Who was just 15 metres away speeding down straight at the three in the car.

"Turn this car." Said Osirus. "It should act as a bump sending him away, but tilt at 25°."

"Pretty decent idea." Said, Shaun.

As approached Atlantas. The three were shocked as it was not only Atlantas but Jules as well.

"You know what, tilt this car perfectly 90 degrees." Advised Osirus.

"It wouldn't work!" Snapped Shaun.

"It scientifically should frickin work." Said Osirus.

"Shut up!" Ranted Shaun.

"Shit, just frickin turn it 90 degrees!" Exclaimed Ernest.

"Urgh! Fine." Sighed Shaun.

As the car turned, exactly came the two. The car wheels screeched through the route. The two came straight at the doors and the window. They struck stiffly straight at the car windows, only to roll off sloping down the route in hard strikes as they collapsed.

As the two collapsed down. Turned the car straight and stopped at as close as 24 metres to the gate.

As the car confronted towards the gate. Came a ginormous sight. At a few metres adjacent. Was a humongous mansion, 2 stories tall with hip roofs along curved endings. As the roof sloped to become wide and spread out.

As the three came. Osirus is in the centre behind Shaun and Ernest Besides him, forward.

"We have to blow this mansion again." Said, Shaun.

"Yeah, it's our often rodeo." Said Ernest "Nothin' special, only special for Osirus."

"Now shut up." Said Osirus lagging, yet in an attempt to appear valiant "Just bang 'em off."

"Fine." Said Shaun and Ernest together.

As only after a second they were surrounded by Assassins round circular. The Assassins were all cocked up to Spears, daggers, Katanas and Kunais. There seemed to be around 450 of them.

At the left was another huge cliff up the main mansion.

While the Assassins were armed. Osirus, Shaun and Ernest weren't. Only Osirus with the good old fountain pen. All dried with blood.

"Bloody hell." Said Shaun calmly "We are done, there's frickin 450 of 'em."

"Wait aren't there fckin 400 of them, how 450?" Asked Osirus.

"We don't have the accurate number." Said Ernest "We don't do surveys."

As the three spoke. Came all the Assassins from every side. Striking Straight at the Three.

Shaun had slammed his tight-ass fist straight into An Assassin, sending him collapsing straight on 30 Assassins. He approached further and kicked every single Assassin, while also dodging getting any backstabs or impales. While Ernest struggled with the slit on his palm yet held on and also ensured Osirus's life. Who was terrified and Could barely impale or stab the pen in any of the Assassins.

Ernest who went straight on booting straight into the huge crowd of Assassins got to hold up to a Katana. As The

Katana got in his hand, he jerked it straight up the throats of the Assassins. It has become chaos for Shaun and Ernest to handle through. While Osirus was tugged over with a whole bunch of Assassins to get Murdered. Where Ernest got cuts every second on his back as he threw each Assassin. Killed each one to save Osirus. Corpses were laying down dead, engulfed with blood, and slits. Whereas Shaun kept on slitting each Assassin. While he was caught hold of from the back.

At an instant time. While Ernest ripped off through the crowd of Assassins injuring him. Osirus was left alone and was Attacked by an Assassin who approached and Sprinted with a Katana along. Injured, blood dried on him yet approaching.

"Crap!" Yelled Osirus anxiously "That guy is coming straight at me."

Osirus squeezed his eyes closed as the Assassin swung his katana to decapitate him. He blacked out. As he opened his eyes. 25 of the Assassins around him lying dead with blood in his arms as he stared at them. Osirus realized what shit happened.

"Oh crap!" Yelled Osirus.

While the Assassins stared at Osirus flabbergasted and intimidated.

"That guy." Said One Assassin "frickin not!"

As Osirus contemplated the acts Anti-genosis committed, wielding his own body. The fountain pen with its tip dripping with blood like molasses.

With Osirus's eyes wide open with guilt and shock. As he dropped the pen down, froze in shock. Anxious with his deeds. Contemplating the slaughter.

"Osirus!" Snapped Ernest "Kill those!"

He came back to reality. With the guilt, he looked at the Assassins with intimidation. As the Assassins moved farther. Came bullets straight at their skulls. As they bled out to death collapsing to the ground.

While Osirus froze, Shaun kicked straight up into Two of The Assassin's skull. As the skulls cracked up, swelling up their foreheads as big as a blister. Then, felt Shaun a slit in his right clavicle. As a Katana impaled in there, deep. He was sent in agony with the blood dripping like a waterfall. He gasped and yelled and placed his hand straight at the Katana as he attempted to remove it only to feel a gun barrel at the right temporal of his skull.

Shaun stroked right, only to see Jules stressing the gun straight.

While got the Katana removed straight out the clavicle, stinging Shaun.

"Ah! These Stupid Assassins." Groaned Shaun.

Jules cocked up his pistol even tighter and said "Scoundrels kill that other guy, don't just stare at him, he can't do shit."

As Jules said that. Ran 4 Assassins straight at Osirus with their Katanas swung at his throat.

"Osirus dawg!" yelled Shaun "Kill!"

As Osirus heard Shaun's yell, he stood up with his fists closed and launched it straight at his right. Sending An Assassin roundhouse collapsing on the ground. While getting attacked by another only suddenly then, came a blue flash straight slamming the Assassins down the route. As they rolled down dead. It was Ernest. With blood splatters on his right cheek and his hand firm tight with a Katana with blood. Looked at Ernest, he murdered the Assassins and rushed on him, even though with injuries. His bandage which had become dirty and covered in blood became tighter than it already was. Ernest had shallow cuts at down his neck, dried out. His left knee with a deep cut. Osirus stared in dead shock at Ernest who caused havoc of bloodshed, well again!

"Bros, how ya do that without any guilt." Whispered Osirus.

"Watch out!"

"Argh!" Snapped Osirus in fear.

Osirus Jerked his right fist tight Cocking up the pen behind. Only to realise was that an Assassin behind who faced his demise by Osirus.

"What the!" Yelled Osirus.

"Shut up!" Said Ernest.

Meanwhile, Shaun, who was outnumbered and held Hostage with a gun pointing at his skull just heard the voice.

"Stupids!" Snapped Jules "I am killing this- ugh (groan)."

As Jules looked down, he could see a dark blue translucent crystal rough blade shoved straight into his belly. Piercing and releasing blood. Jules's eyes opened wide as he groaned in agonizing pain.

"M..mother-"

Shaun booted Jules straight up, sending him impacting the other two Assassins as Jules rolled down at the gate.

After a few seconds, the other Assassins jerked their weapons straight at Ernest. He slammed a flying kick straight on the Assassins, breaking their skulls.

Shaun Who was free jerked up a roundhouse kick straight at the other 2 Assassins left and all the 450 Assassins were left dead. However, though, Shaun and Ernest were injured. They had slits, wounds and hits blown on them. The two walked slowly and moved unstable of injuries while gasping for breath after killing off 450

Assassins.

Meanwhile, Osirus left in Shock of that he survived.

"Come." Said Ernest.

"yeah fine." Gasped Osirus.

The three approached inside the mansion. Empty shallow without any person.

"I'm bringin' explosives." Said, Shaun.

"You are bringing what!" Snapped Osirus in shock.

"Yeah." Said Shaun "I bought it while you two bastards were kicking each other's ass and I was fixing the car."

"Where did you get those?" Questioned Osirus.

"I stole 'em from some local gangsters in our area."

"We were living close to frickin gangsters!" Snapped Osirus.

"Shut up don't shout!" Whispered Shaun in frustration.

As they checked. There was no Assassin. But was loaded up with Spears, Katanas, daggers and Kunai.

"Wait I am coming with the explosives." Said, Shaun.

"Fine." Said Ernest.

"They will be coming anytime."

"Yeah I know, but we've been blowing this up for a long time and always helps." Said Ernest "Even though there's no one here. It works as an inventory to get weapons for backup."

"So we blowing this house up."

"Yeah."

"Then we gotta take one weapon." Suggested Osirus.

"Why would you?" Asked Ernest.

"To fight them." Said Osirus.

"My guy." Laughed Ernest "They are the best for killing them, you can't kill one guy without powers or anxiety, you'll just f things up."

"Bloody I won't." Said Osirus.

"Why, why I mean why would you frickin need a spear when it's going to be no help to you?" questioned Ernest "You are gonna f up without this spear, you will f up with this spear. Any difference, nope."

"(sigh) I won't murder with it. I will shove it up in their butt-."

"No, You can't." Said Ernest "It will not be operateable for you. You while swishing it once in the air will be killed by the Assassins. You won't even have your remaining teeth left."

"Argh! Just let me just..... take it." Said Osirus.

"Ahh! Fine take it, don't be a pain in the ass. Already these Assassins are a pain in my ass, I ain't your mom after all!" Annoyed Ernest.

"Lemme take this then." Said Osirus.

As he cocked up a spear with a sharp pointed blade Along with a Hollow hole round and wide like an iris. Easy to murder anyone with a brute. The spear had curves around its blade and the down handle of the blade was designed with motifs coloured gold and the other part, matte smooth grey till the down with a curve at the down. It seemed perfect for a 5'9 foot tall Osirus to wield as it towered up to the height of 6 feet.

"I am taking this one." Said Osirus "Seems great."

"Only if it helps."

"Yeah, whatever." Said Osirus moving his eyes around.

Then came Shaun with the heavy explosives in both of his fists held tight.

"hush.." gasped Shaun keeping the explosives down.

"Yeah now place it quick." Said Ernest.

As Ernest and Shaun dragged the Explosives at the weapons. Came a strong explosion straight at them from a window sending wood particles flying around. Shaun,

Ernest and Osirus impacted and crashed hard a few metres back the explosives.

"Argh! (Panting) Shit!!" Groaned Osirus.

"(gasps) Ah shit." Whispered Shaun.

The three of them were all injured. Ernest and Shaun had blood from their cheeks coming from their chest and neck. Ernest's right cheek was cut deep with blood. While Shaun's left cheek was all charred and numb. A wooden piece impaled close into his right kidney releasing blood.

Osirus was fortunate. Who Only had redness and a burning sensation on his left-sided face.

As stood agonized Ernest. He could see a huge sharp hole with looked at far, was an Assassin with a round barrelled rocket launcher, exhaling hot smoke. With the barrel hot at the end.

Then came suddenly An Assassin flying down straight At Ernest. He struck straight at Ernest. Kicking his chest. Slamming Ernest straight rubbing down to the wooden floor. Producing sparks.

Then, the Assassin struck straight at Osirus. Cocking up a dagger. As he moved straight at him. He was crashed straight by Shaun's Shoulder's impact on the ground. The Assassin rose, only to get booted hard on his chest by Shaun towards the wall. Along with his head hitting the staircase. Breaking his fall hard.

As stood the Assassin to speed up against Shaun. Came out the bloody red particles and electricity with a glow as he swung at high speed. As he approached the halfway. He sensed a huge rip in his throat all of a sudden, he stopped. The sight he could see was his body without a head collapsing and a spear in the air held by the fists of Osirus.

Osirus had decapitated him.

The Assassin was nothing, dead.

The tip had blood flowing down as it covered the spearhead with blood as dark as molasses.

Osirus couldn't understand what he just did.

"What the hell just happened?" Asked Osirus as he stood. Shaun stood stern and surprised as he murdered an Assassin with a weapon that seemed unusable to him. So was Ernest, he too stood frozen in contemplation.

As Osirus stared at the Spearhead. He was terrified and threw the spear in filth as he stared at the decapitated corpse.

"Shit." Subdued Osirus in shock "What the heck did I do."

"Osirus, come we have more Assassins to take down, stay strong." Groaned Ernest.

"Ah! Imposter syndrome cut it!" Snapped Shaun "I'll leave none of your life alive, just get your Butt up."

"Fine." Sighed Osirus as he was disgusted and intimidated.

As Stood Osirus, they decided to leave.

As the three walked. Sensed Shaun that the Assassin loading up the Rocker launcher and pointing them straight.

"Shit." Rushed Shaun "Run!"

As the three rushed out. Osirus, who was sprinting his life along his spear, could feel caught by his jacket. As he looked back was Shaun.

"What are you doing?" Hissed Osirus.

"Wait." Said, Shaun.

Shaun caught and threw Osirus straight a few metres wide. Osirus as he collapsed straight on back along his spear with a huge impact could feel anything but good. His back as it agonized resisted him to cock up Stern up the ground. As he was left with an agonizing backache.

As came running Shaun and Ernest. A huge blast came straight into the mansion. Blowing the mansion up. The wood all spread out in small sharp pieces and it was a huge explosion that blew up the two explosives. Sending Shaun and Ernest 4 metres fast. But fortunate for them, no wood impaled or shock impact. Only Shaun with the early Wooden piece impale. While Osirus was sent his head aching. His sound nerves which were shocked with a huge burst of noise were all overcharged.

As blew the Mansion, all that came into sight were the remains of the mansion engulfed in flames, burning them down.

As Shaun and Ernest sighted the cliff from where the Assassin shot the rocket launcher. He wasn't there.

"Ah, crap." Said Shaun "He's coming here."

"Let's sprint and open that damn gate up." Said Ernest.

"Take this dawg up." Said Shaun "He looks like he has had a stroke or something."

"Yeah wait lemme bring him."

Ernest walked towards Osirus who was lying down like dead.

"Bro, come fast." Said Ernest.

"I am having mahogany of a headache." Sighed Osirus As he held his forehead in Agony.

"Fine, just stand up." Said Ernest.

"Seriously Idiot." Said Osirus as he sighted sternly at Ernest.

"You big pile of shit, come up fast, that bazooka guy's coming to bang us again!" Said Ernest "This time from the front."

"Then let's just return." Said Osirus "What are we gonna do if he's coming from the front."

"Kill him with tactics." Said Ernest "Super Bloody easy."

"(sigh) fine Idiot!" Shouted Osirus.

Osirus held up to Ernest's hand and stood.

As he looked around Shaun appeared stern.

"Let's go now." Said Shaun "But don't crash straight into it."

As the three walked close to the ginormous gate, they hid beside the gates, at the walls. Shaun and Ernest who decided to sense the Assassin camped along Osirus who stood by Ernest.

"You guys scare me." Whispered Osirus.

"That's the thing we have to deal with, not a first rodeo." Said Ernest.

As tried Ernest and Shaun to sense An Assassin. They couldn't sense one.

"What the hell." Said Ernest "Are they holding all the Assassins at the base."

"Seems tho." Said, Shaun.

"Let's frickin go then." Whispered Osirus.

"Yeah." Said Ernest "wield a shield."

"Wait, how?" Asked Osirus.

"I don't know, find out yourself or stay behind."

"I'm staying behind."

Osirus backed as he cocked up to his spear.

As Ernest and Shaun came close to the gate and were about to leave their hand to open up the gate. Came a huge shock. An explosion, sending Shaun and Ernest bombarded a few metres away and high up in the sky. As the gate petrified and reduced to dust, the wood particles spread out. Osirus felt another mahogany of a headache, even worse. Sending him on the ground with his nerves popping up.

While Ernest landed straight on his back. Feeling pain through his spinal cord and ribs. The bandage loosened open and what could be seen was another of a wound.

While Shaun could feel a huge weight on his head as he stood. He felt nausea. He could feel his vision wobbly as he stared around. As the three sighted behind the reduced particles gate. Was the Assassin with his rocket launcher. With a melted barrel that shot huge explosions out.

"Holy shit!" Shouted Osirus in shock "This guy!"

"Wait." Said Ernest as he stood stern along the shield as the Assassin aimed towards him.

"Shit." Whispered Shaun as he witnessed.

As the Assassin pulled the trigger, came another blow. It struck straight at Ernest's shield as he wielded it in front. Sending him Slamming back.

"Take this guy down!" Exclaimed Shaun as he replenished a blade out of his fists.

He showered straight at the Assassin. Impaling in his Solar plexus, sending him into Agony. Ernest, who crashed on the ground stood and threw his shield hard straight aiming at the Assassin. The shield slammed. Sending the Assassin on the ground.

The Assassin as he stood holding his anvil was struck straight as came Shaun. The Assassin, as he sighted straight into Shaun's brown eyes, donned with Blues. The Assassin gasping for breath could feel his vision blurred and pain in his belly. As looked down a blue blade impaled, opening up a flow of blood moving out. The next moment was the impaled blade dragged out, sending the Assassin clutching up to his agonized belly as he stared was Shaun's right hand's fingers painted rough with blood as dark as thick tomato paste.

Shaun struck his blade straight at the Assassin's throat, sprinting towards him.

As came the blade closed his eye. Shaun stopped. Shaun froze sternly as red nerves visible seen in his eyes. Down he stared was the hand of the Assassin pressing down the wood piece impaled down. As it approached it's way deeper.

Then the Assassin as he slammed his forehead on Shaun. Had sent him in agony, gasping for breath.

As Shaun approached his head down, he saw the Assassin. The Assassin was blown by a huge ice blow, with translucent drippy icy spikes breaking like grass at his chest. Sending the Assassin metres back. Letting go of Shaun.

As Shaun crutched up the wooden piece pierced into his belly, the blood flew out.

The Assassin, thrown on the ground stood. Incepted sprinting, having the grudge to take the three down.

As he sped up holding up a dagger.

As the Assassin approached, came Sprinting Ernest. As he caught hold of his dagger-donned arm. All sudden & Swift came a huge forehead crash, straight on Ernest's Forehead. Injuring him, as the skull agonized. He squeezed his eyes, feeling something like a brain freeze as he stared up with a blurry vision as his nerves closed his eyes popped like a stick and spun like a ball tip in a ball pen as used for writing.

As he looked was pain and blood flowing as the dagger impaled in Ernest's Solar plexus Releasing blood.

Looked at Ernest, his eyes as red nerves popping. Gasping for breath as he lost Oxygen and blood slowly.

Then came running Shaun as he booted crashing the Assassin down. Leaving Ernest impaled as the dagger created a slit for the blood to draw out. As he collapsed down to the ground.

Shaun clinched up the throat of the Assassin with all the power he could use. Until, suddenly getting booted by him. Shaun jerked up as he stood. His eyes popped with red nerves, furious.

The Assassin who was about to stand.

Was sighted in rage as Shaun yelled. Swinging his left arm.

"Slît kânthahà!" Yelled Shaun.

As swung the arm. The Assassin could feel passing out slowly. His throat burning. His blood dripping down his robes. As the blood appeared maroon. Looked at, was his throat slit, as the blood flew.

He was dead. Collapsing on the ground.

Shaun gasped for breath. His eyes widened as he inhaled air each second.

Osirus stared intimidated as he saw something he didn't expect.

"What the hell." Spoke Osirus "Such a thing was possible?" As he stared in confusion.

"Only if you knew and were not living under a boulder." Gasped Shaun.

"Ernest looks heck skewered." Said Osirus.

"Yeah, I know."

The two walked towards Ernest, who was in agony as blood came and the dagger deep in gave a pinch every second. His eyes closed and strained like stuck in a jacket zip as he was in pain. He gasped as he probably never had.

"Arghh." Gasped Ernest "It pains, heck a lot."

"Yeah stand now." Said Shaun taking heavy breaths.

"Yeah wait let me just remove this thing out of me."

As he dragged the dagger out. He groaned in agony. As the dagger came out, the blood flew out like syringed hot sauce. Finally came the dagger out. Ernest panted for breath as he placed both his hands on the impale. Drying and patching it up. Only until what remained was dried, stiff skin looking like blood.

"Finally." Sighed Ernest as he stood up relieved.

"Now let's bust 'em up." Said Shaun "They are camping up."

"We'll bust?" Asked Osirus "We can sneak in."

"No, we can't." Said Shaun "This ain't a fort or two. They aren't kings, powerful than one though."

"Also, Idiots." Questioned Osirus "If you could slit throats, why wouldn't you do that in the first place?"

"It doesn't work how you asking about it." Said Shaun "It's a difficult thing to do, it backfires."

"You mean you can commit suicide?" Asked Osirus.

"No, murder." Said Shaun "On anyone except the one meant for."

"Ah, then why did you even use it?"

"If didn't, we would've been wasting our energy plus it's not even that scary."

"Fine." Sighed Osirus.

"Now let's go." Said Ernest "You both wasting a lot of time, let's go now before we are reduced to ashes."

"Yeah." Said, Shaun.

The trio walked up towards it. As they noticed were no Assassins there, no one to disrupt.

As the sun set complete. The sky is navy blue. Empty without the moon. No stars.

All it was darkness arising.

On the top reached Shaun, Ernest and Osirus. Looked at was a huge land. With grass terrains, roughs and rocks. There were trees to be looked at. Fences round. A small hut, weapon house and stared at the front was a humongous mansion. Three stories tall. Hip curved roofs.

"Holy shit." Said Osirus "How is this thing not yapped about."

"What do you mean?" Asked Shaun.

"I mean why are no Satellites not finding out about it." Said Osirus.

"They have their ways to resist it." Said Ernest.

"Okay." Said Osirus.

The three stopped in front of the huge mansion. With 10 metres away being a huge pit. Dug filled up along the water. Right-sided was a huge not deep pit. Waterlogged.

The closer they walked. Assassins came out, Handled with spears, daggers and katanas.

Then Came out four formidable Assassins.

Bludreth, Thraxor, Sangorath and Sirius. All with their eyes red death staring. Mouth covered in the shades of a mask.

Bludreth as he wielded his kunai in both hands. Aimed at the three.

Thraxor. Holding up a huge reaver axe both his hands at the handle as he wielded it pointing Ernest to the side.

Sangorath, wielding a dagger stiff his right fist. As he waited for a movement.

Sirius had an A24 holding his Right arm. As he kept it up facing the air.

All four were covered in black clothing and a thick dark grey vest. Armed with weapons in their bunch of pockets up their black cargo.

Surrounding were Assassins, all armed up.

"Give me the spear." Said, Shaun.

Shaun instantly snatched the Spear, wielding in Osirus's arm. As he pointed it straight up threatening.

Osirus as he took his pen out and Ernest, forming an ice blade.

Then came down the stairs, Javon. Wearing black robes. A hood up his head, Along with the cape floating and wavering up the wind. His hair wavering. He came out as he stared at the three dead still. Without saying anything.

He dragged a cigarette out of his pocket. Placing it in his mouth. As it was placed, lit up red. Smoke came out.

Shaun stared still at Javon. Jerked the spear straight at Javon's throat. As he applied his energy and strength. It didn't do any wonders. The spear and his hand stopped as red particles flew by.

Only for Shaun to get pushed hard.

After that Shaun attempted to move. He was stuck and froze as he tried sprinting. So was Ernest, they both were frozen. While Javon giggled as he looked at them.

"Capture." Mumbled Javon.

As Osirus stood in shock looking at his friends froze. While his friends struggled to move.

"What the heck," said Shaun.

"Something's skewered." Said Ernest "skewered."

As they both had bad gut feelings. They became true. As they sensed something not very great.

While Osirus stood too, sensed something. As he tried moving, he too was frozen stiff his movement. And then all of a sudden, came a huge breeze of Red particles coming from his back.

"Osirus! Back out!" Yelled Ernest.

The next moment Osirus heard Ernest's yell, and came a huge strike. A hard and painful strike straight at his parietal. As it struck straight hard at him. Making him dizzy and sending him in shock. As his brain felt heavy. He was sent with the pain. Osirus covered it with his right hand and as he saw it it was blood. The next moment, where flows of blood came down as he looked behind was Jules, cocking up a spade, with its blade covered in blood. Osirus gasped as he could feel his breath going away.

Only to sight Atlantas appearing up his eyes, teleported. Along a dagger. Impaling straight up his belly. As blood Came out.

While Shaun and Ernest are in shock.

"Shit!!" Screamed Both Shaun and Ernest.

They both were free as they attempted to attack, only to get beaten up by a huge herd of Assassins. As Atlantas dragged out the dagger was Osirus, gasping for breath as he collapsed down to the ground, unconscious.

"Shit!" Yelled Ernest.

As the two tried moving. They both were slammed straight on their forehead. They were then attacked by a huge herd of Assassins. Smacking them hard. After a while, all they looked like were injured and messed up.

As they stared in agony, Sangorath dragged Osirus up his shoe. Only to throw him up the back pit. As they crashed the unconscious Osirus straight into the pit of water.

The blood dyed the water red in an instant.

As the two watched in agony. Only to be smacked hard. The two were unconscious and wrecked.

CHAPTER EIGHT

Osirus was dead. That could be thought of looking at him, his body loose, floating up the water.

Upfront the pit was the spear impaled in the ground, deep.

Meanwhile, Javon was busy opening the box inside the three-story tall mansion. They only had 5,000 layers left. All it looked like was a thin box.

The shields became thinner than they ever were.

Shaun and Ernest up the floor. They were tied up to a long wooden log.

As Shaun opened his eyes, Javon was pumping smoke and the cigarette butt sucked up in his lips.

"(gasps) Argh!" Shaun whispered in pain.

Shaun could feel a bunch of sharp objects impaled on his back. It sent him feeling extremely stinging as he attempted to move in front. He felt a bundle of spikes picking out his whole back. Shaun was in extreme pain, he realised that back him. The log was carved with spikes. It was impaling him. His blood was stuck in the spikes.

"Argh! Holy cow!" Groaned Shaun as he stared up at Javon.

As he looked beside his right was Ernest, blood-dried and unconscious. Shaun continued staring. He saw a piece of blade impaled straight into his left knee.

Ernest was looking terrible.

As he jerked his neck front, Javon was in front. He pumped the smoke straight into Shaun's face.

"That dog was conscious as we dragged his butt up. He was outnumbered so Frickin bad." Spoke Javon "It was such a thing stabbing him."

"Shut up." Groaned Shaun.

"You pop your ears out." Said Javon as he threw the cigarette on Shaun "Your stupid trio is gonna be eaten up by me as I grasp every single nutrient of you, your shitty powers, that third Bastard is dead and anyways that Anti-genosis is Narcissistic, didn't help him."

"Why are you telling me this? Huh?" Groaned Shaun.

"Cause you found a crappy guy to get help from." Said Javon "Genosis just finds some dipshit people instead of a proper wielder."

"Shut up." Whispered Shaun.

"Fine, whatever floats your boat." Sighed Javon as he walked towards the box, continuing to open it.

Meanwhile, outside the base. The Assassins were all packed, cocked up to spears and daggers. Jules, Atlantas, Bludreth, Thraxor and Sangorath surrounded the front of the base holding up A24's in their hands.

While in the pit, all of a sudden. Moved a finger. They were throwing up the breeze of water. They were Followed by, moving fingers over fingers. The water lit as it glowed violet.

Out of the water came a leg as it drooled the water out. On the front came a hand out of the pit. Both hands as they gripped out the pit. Then swung out Osirus. Wet as the blood-coloured water dripped out of the body. Looked at him, blood dripped. The hair clustered. Osirus with no emotions as he stared dead still in front.

As the Assassins saw, they cocked their guns up, aiming at Osirus. As they stared at him, they realised, it wasn't the coward and weak Osirus they took down. It was **Antigenosis. Alter!**

"That guy has come out." Said Sangorath "It's difficult taking him down if it's Genosis."

"Take him down!" yelled Thraxor.

"Telè." Whispered Alter.

As the Assassins pulled Trigger, disappeared Alter and the spear. Sending the bullets speeding far down the forest.

"That guy is Armed now." Said Sangorath.

"Where is Sirius?" Asked Bludreth.

"Doozing around with guns & his disciples probably." Said Sangorath "I wonder how he fits all of them in that small Arsenal hut."

As they talked a body flying as it crashed straight up Sangorath's eyes.

As they looked behind, Alter had cocked up the spear as he ripped the chest off the Assassin.

An Assassin came running straight up Osirus. He swung his hand up Alter. Only for the hand to be clutched up by him, he slammed the Assassin straight to the ground, cocking up the arm as the ankle joint cracked up.

Only until Alter smashed his left leg up the Assassin's head, he died with the skull cracked inside.

As Alter left the Assassin, came a huge herd of them. He spun his spear round, hitting the spear butt up every Assassin. He stabbed the spear butt straight up an Assassin's belly. Alter swiftly dragged the spear out. As he did. Came bullets flying straight at him. As the five main Assassins fired at him. He teleported straight back, saying Telè.

As he came back, he could feel his neck dragged by an Assassin, he was rocketed up the sky. Alter acted suddenly as he penetrated the Spear up the Assassin's chest and he soon clinched up the Assassin. As he crashed into the Assassin. He threw him straight at Atlantas and Jules. They fell hard. Alter ran up. He was surrounded by a crowd of Assassins. They busted on him. He impaled his spear up Assassin's chests. Blood flew and splattered. He was injured too. He was slammed hard on the ground as he would be smacked and punched to the ground. He slammed kicks upon kicks to the Assassins who were wrestling upon him.

As Alter stood. He swung out particles Magenta sending the Assassin's slamming on the ground. As he walked up the. He thrusted the spear in the Four Assassins's stomachs. The spear impaling slower and heavier. He quickly dragged the thrust Spear out, blood dripping like sweat from the spear blade.

From Behind, he sensed an Assassin sprinting up. Alter ran up, and he swung the spear straight up. The spear swung, and it went through fast. Looked at, it had penetrated through the Assassin's head. The head now drilled up as a rough hole, with blood splattering. Alter removed the Spear from the ripped face. It already had blood flowing down. As he looked up down the water pit. He had his blood dried.

He then stared at Mansion, as he sensed the box. As he looked, All the Assassins realised his intentions they ran up, attempting to block him.

Alter realised it and ran adrenaline fast. Sweat fell behind, mixing with the blood-bathed grass.

"Stupids." Whispered Alter.

He slammed straight up the Assassins. As they flew by. Blood started coming out. It turned out that Alter impaled the spear swiftly upon the Assassins.

As Alter moved. Throats slit, Assassin's flew up, skulls & ribs broke. Finally, after Alter had taken down a huge herd of Assassins. Then Sangorath came erect in, clinching up a rocket launcher. As he pulled the trigger.

Alter suddenly wielded a shield. It blew him up in the air. Sending him rolling behind. Hitting the filthy blood-bathed grass.

As Alter stood, came an instant slit up the back. As he looked behind was Thraxor holding up a huge heavy axe.

Only for Alter to kick him, sending Thraxor down the grass.

As looked Alter behind came another blow from Sangorath. Sending him blown up in the air. As he stared up, came Jules, Atlantas and Bludreth tugging him. They jerked up daggers. Alter held them and blew them high up in the air. They slammed strong, metres away from the ground. Shaking their brains away.

As he stared around, Sangorath came running up to him. Alter ran swiftly, leaving the blood-covered grass behind. Sangorath threw up the Rocket launcher, slamming straight on Osirus's puppeted body. He fell hard.

❧❧❧

Meanwhile, Javon. Who had already opened 2,365 layers of the box. Was alerted about the behemoth happening.

"(Giggles) That guy is alive." Said Javon "Would be a phenomenal wagyu to hunt down."

"Cannibal piece of crap, It ain't Osirus, it's Genosis." Said, Shaun.

"Doesn't matter." Said Javon "You know Ernest is Overcharged and that's why he's like that and got beaten to shit."

"So why are you telling me that when Osirus is coming." Said, Shaun.

"Cause he's pre-cooking himself for me." Said Javon "You know what I mean, right."

"Argh, crap." Whispered, "That Unemployed dawg should use his brain, get the Genosis out, controlling his body."

"Ain't happening, not literate enough to do it." Said Javon as he continued opening the box up.

Meanwhile, Sangorath smacked a strong kick up Alter. Sending him crashing down to the ground, the skull shook, Osirus's brain heavy. As soon as he stood his butt up, he was bombarded with punches. Smashing into his nose. Then suddenly Alter caught firm hold of the fist, and he slammed Sangorath out of his way. Alter dragged the spear up his fists as he ran towards the base.

Suddenly came Thraxor and Bludreth as they both were armed with katanas.

Alter slammed a huge kick to blow up the two as they swung their katanas up Osirus.

Alter, blocked the attacks as he swung up the Opposite sides.

The farther they moved, the more closer they came to the pit.

As they reached close to the pit. Alter got his collar dragged. As he got clutched up his collar by Atlantas. He held him, leaving Thraxor and Bludreth Impaling the katanas up Osirus's belly.

Blood flew quickly, and Osirus drooled it out of his mouth the next quick moment.

As the two removed the Katanas from his belly, they crashed down the grass as Alter kicked them fast. As the two fell, Alter jerked his right ankle up Atlantas's Solar plexus. Sending him down the pit.

As ran Osirus, he had his leg clutched up by Sangorath and crashed him down the grass.

As soon As Alter crashed, Sangorath had his face smacked by Osirus's sneaker sole. Sending Sangorath clutching up his face, he was in pain.

Then, Alter stood, and he jumped front running fast upfront, the winds thrashed, yet couldn't do anything.

As Alter reached close to the mansion, he was crashed into by the Assassins. They kicked, punched, head-butted upon him.

Alter smacked out a kick strong. Sending Assassins flew far.

As Assassins upon Assassins kept bursting out.

Dead, skewered and blood-dried.

Alter caught hold of the spear.Stabbing it into Assassins. Ripped, broken and dead. As Alter swung his spear all out. At last, all that was left were corpses, injured Assassins and Osirus/Alter. As he hobbled up the mansion.

As he entered the door. Came a strike straight at his shoulder from the right, looked at was Jules. He dragged out the knife, only to impale it straight in Osirus's belly. Skewering blood out the belly, sending the body panicking.

Osirus's body came down to the knees. As he drooled blood from his mouth. The spear as it loosened up from the fists, slowly sliding down.

"This guy is dead." Said Jules.

"Howdy." Groaned Alter "I wanted to Spill some cashews out my mouth."

"What do you have to Spill out." Said Jules "Just spill your last cashews out."

"It's that." Whispered Alter "Crèk kânthahà."

"You mother-" Jules could feel his nerves as they swung and broke. His neck cracked.

As Jules looked around, he couldn't hear anything and felt like zoning out.

"Now you are dead." Whispered Alter and swung the spear straight at Jules's throat, penetrating through. The blood dripped slowly, his eyes widened, his mouth opened, and his body turned cold and pale.

Jules was dead.

As the Spear came out. The corpse collapsed.

Looked front came Assassins. As They kicked Osirus down the floor.

They all tugged down Osirus. As they attempted stabbing daggers. While Alter kicked them away. As they flew by.

Alter crashed kick on each. The more he fought, the more tiring and difficult it became.

As he stood up to his knees. He was stabbed up his back. It was Atlantas who did it. As Alter attempted jerking up. The more the dagger impaled in. Osirus was stuck frozen. As he froze, came from the front sangorath. Who impaled the spear up Osirus's belly. Penetrating all the way through. The organs fought hard, losing blood and slowly dying out.

As the spear impaled. Ejected out violet particles around the collar. It was Osirus back to his consciousness. As he stared 'round. He had a blurry vision as he gasped for breath, he almost felt like death. Losing breath, the heart pumping slower. Losing consciousness.

He Groaned vomiting sounds as he gasped and felt the agony.

He could feel his fat, artilleries skewered and messed up. As blood came out in no time.

But As Osirus looked, all he could do was see but, couldn't hear anything.

As the situation couldn't get any worse, Sangorath dragged the spear quickly out.

As blood swiftly came out. Osirus could feel himself blacking out. The Organs dying faster.

In no time, Osirus was shut and still as his jaw droppeddown.

All that happened was blood drooling out his mouth.

"Douche is dead." Gasped Sangorath as he slammed up the spear straight to the floor "He is dead."

They laughed & chuckled as slowly as they could with all the breath left.

Suddenly, Osirus's lips bit.

As the dagger came out Osirus fell. He remained stood up on his knees. He showed a rapid moment.

"tèlè." Whispered Alter and Osirus simultaneously.

Then suddenly surrounding Osirus's body came particles and the next moment the particles flew out. Osirus was there no more.

"Oh crap." Said Sangorath "It's Genosis, Again."

suddenly, Osirus crashed straight at Sangorath, from the back.

They both slammed hard. Alter caught hold of the spear and swung it against all the Assassins.

As they stood far. Alter smashed his right leg up Sangorath's head. He applied pressure. The wooden floor creaked even more. Sangorath then pushed a strong kick.

"Ah, fudge." Said Bludreth.

Alter then dragged his leg out as he approached close to a Wall, wooden. He began rubbing up his sneakers to the wall. The Assassins were stern as he rubbed the wall. Suddenly, Sparks came out. Dripping down the ground. As they turned pink. Catching fire. He quickly removed the leg from the wall.

The fire came up fast. Then Alter crashed a kick straight at Atlantas sending him off the walls, he collapsed, rolling down the grass.

As Alter ran straight at the staircase, he was slammed with a push by Thraxor and he dragged Osirus. Throwing him up the weapons.

As came Thraxor running. Sat Alter as he waved his hands up himself. At the next moment. He was slammed hard out the wall. The wooden pieces flew out to the grass. A huge Hole formed. He was stuck inside the hole. His half-body was swinging out. Floating and pressed up to sharp wood.

Suddenly, he got dragged in his legs as Thraxor stabbed a Dagger Swift up his solar plexus. Each time he stabbed, the more blood came out.

It had become a mess around. Blood everywhere.

Osirus's body was all injured. Thraxor threw his dagger down. He cocked up a Glock and pointed straight up Osirus's chest.

Osirus Stood looks up at Thraxor. As he clutched his stomach up his arms. Even though Alter didn't get any damage. He could feel the heaviness of his existence.

As Thraxor pulled the trigger. The Bullet stuck straight up to Osirus's chest. As Genosis controlling Osirus looked up. He slammed a stiff kick up Thraxor. Sending him up the flame-engulfed wall. The bullet came off the chest, it didn't even manage to make a scratch to the chest.

By that moment, all the walls were engulfed in flames. They began reaching up.

Alter stared up the stairs. He could see the fire catching up to them.

As Alter saw it. He sped straight up the Staircase. But he was quickly slammed down to the ground by Sangorath, Bludreth and Atlantas who tugged on him.

Thraxor pointed to The Gun. The barrel faced up Osirus's parietal part or the skull.

The further Alter crawled. The more Thraxor pressed down the trigger.

The other Three Assassins impaled up daggers, the back of Osirus and clinched up to him as tight as they could.

"Thin kid." Gasped Thraxor "Don't be cocky. I will blow your brains out."

"When was I.... Cocky?" Said Genosis as a though coarse voice came "You are the ones being cocky."

"Shut up." Snapped Thraxor.

"As you wish stupid." Said Anti-Genosis "Then I'll make sure this place goes to shit."

Suddenly, Osirus's body disappeared. Leaving magenta particles behind.

As Thraxor looked around. He was smashed down the ground. He could feel his head pressed down to the ground. As the wooden floor creaked.

Alter slammed Thraxor down, kicking the Glock away.

Suddenly, Sangorath Swung a punch straight, and it crashed straight up Osirus's face. He slammed punch over punch. As Osirus's face kept slamming. The more the philtrum below became dark. Only until, Alter slammed a kick up Sangorath. Sending him back. As he rolled up to the other Assassins. Alter stood Gasping for breath as he tightened up his fists.

All the Assassin's stood wild as Alter walked front wounded up the right leg.

The first floor was all engulfed in flames, The staircase too caught flames up the sides. As the stairs began breaking. Alter ran as fast as he could. Breaking off the stairs as he ran. As he came up to the first floor, there were Assassins armed up to Katanas. As he aimed the spear to be thrown. It was instantly thrown by the swung Katans of the Assassins.

As they aimed their katanas up Osirus. Came a barrel pointed up Osirus's skull. Looked around and saw red particles. It was Sangorath, aiming up the Glock barrel up the skull.

Sangorath pushed up the gun close To Osirus's parietal harder.

He clinched up the trigger, close to being fully pressed.

"Dead, now." Said Sangorath.

"(Giggles) Well... I suggest-"

"You suggest what huh?" Said Sangorath.

"I suggest you reconsider this decision. Cause well... it's shit." Said Alter.

"Well, now a kid will teach me." Said Sangorath "Shut up with your Yapping."

Alter swiftly slammed Osirus's elbow up Sangorath's Solar plexus. Sending Sangorath back. Alter swiftly cocked up a katana up his arms. Sangorath pulled the trigger. As the bullet came so swung the katana. As the bullet hit the katana. It was cut. Split apart. It looked like electric sparks. As the split bullets passed by Osirus's ears. Just besides. Falling to the ground.

As soon as the bullet hit the ground. Alter jerked the Katana up Sangorath's glock. As it struck the glock. The barrel flew out.

Suddenly, the Other Assassins ran up as they wielded their katanas.

Alter slammed up a strong kick up an Assassin. As he smacked one punch on another one. Until he swung the katana. All that was seen was blood.

As Alter swung his katana around. It impaled in many. Until a dagger struck him in the back. As blood started dripping, Burning sensations kicked in.

Looked behind was Sangorath, as he pushed in the dagger more. Nerves were skewering. Blood was dripping. The spine was just close to being skewered. As the dagger came out, the blood dripped and flew out fast.

As Alter turned around, he was stern as he held tight up the dagger, only to swing it up Osirus's belly. But Alter caught hold of the dagger as he stared sternly into Sangorath's Eyes. Alter snatched up the dagger and he threw it away the left wall.

Alter walked back as he pointed the Katana up Sangorath. At the chest.

"Reconsider." Said Sangorath "Will go in vain."

"Tis 'but a scratch, not even messing round."

"Big loss for that Scoundrel though." Said Atlantas low-toned.

Looked behind. Atlantas held up a dagger around Osirus's throat.

"Better shut up being a pain in the butt, or this animal you living in will be reduced to atoms, that matters to you, Right?" He continued.

"Come back?" Asked Alter.

"I will reduce this fat piece of crap to atoms- Argh!"

The Katana was impaled by Alter, as he penetrated it through his belly. The blood came out. Skewering, as Alter dragged out the Katana.

Blood flew down as he Groaned clutching up to his stomach.

As the Assassins saw it, they weren't dead still anymore. They all ran up, holding up their katanas as they swung the Katanas to kill Osirus.

As they came. Alter Jerked up the Katana straight at One Assassin. It Thrust inside one's intestines. He swiftly took the Katana out and swung it straight at one's throat. Sending the Assassin down off.

Then he slammed the Katana straight into another Assassin's knee.

As soon as Alter removed the Katana. He was slammed hard on the staircase by Atlantas.

The staircase is strongly built. Broke the impact rough. Making the spine feel wobbly and displaced. His legs were all stretched out as he sat down on the floor. His abdomen slanted up the stairs as if resting on the chair.

All the Assassins pointed the Katana up to him as if at any moment they might cut his throat.

Then came walking Atlantas stern as his fists appeared closed tight.

He grabbed the collar of Osirus's black t-shirt as he stared sternly into his eyes. He kneeled up as he came close.

"The hell you looking at?" Said Genosis barely audible.

"Your Life done for." Said Atlantas.

He brought out a dagger and he pressed it up Osirus's throat.

"Stop." Said Sangorath.

Atlantas took his dagger back.

"What?"

"Just cut open the throat man, Don't do extra bullshit."

"Fine."

Then Atlantas clinched hard up the dagger's handle as he was about to swing it. Before he could do it. He was swiftly slammed with a kick by Osirus. Straight at his schlong. Sending Atlantas sliding up the floor.

"Holy crap." Groaned Atlantas.

Alter Stood swiftly and then took a huge jump. He slammed through all the Assassins. As he slammed down the wooden floor. Up his eyes was his spear.

He swiftly cocked up the Spear. Rolling up.

The fire had already engulfed the walls round.

Alter swiftly smashed the Spear butt down the floor. Breaking a hole open.

An Assassin came Running as he slammed a kick up Osirus's chest. Sending Osirus down the floor, Slammed.

He swiftly got up and smashed the Spear butt closing the eyebrow and eye of the Assassin, Slamming him down.

Alter swiftly smashed a kick on the Assassins. Sending them to the wooden floor. The floor creaked, as the Assassins slowly stood up and turned The spear swiftly. But the Spear was Slammed Away by Thraxor, As he slammed a kick. Smashing Osirus stiff the Staircase.

Alter could feel Osirus's body all damaged.

As he sensed the blood to the nape.

Alter stood as he shook and struggled to stand normally.

Thraxor Swiftly smashed his right Elbow straight into Alter's chest. Slamming him down to the Ground.

Alter couldn't cope with the fact that Osirus's body's condition made it difficult to even stand up with legs.

As he approached further up. He was slammed down the stairs again by Thraxor.

By That point, Genosis himself felt tired. He felt it heavy to teleport off there. Osirus was doomed it seemed like.

Meanwhile, Javon pumping out smoke. As he sucked up the chemicals of the cigarette in his mouth. Opening the box. The box by that time was all but a floating red ball. Blocked by very thin grids. Very close to being removed. They appeared around 4cm the width. All that was left were 2,000 layers to be removed.

Shaun stared All tired and weak. As Javon Continued Opening the box, the cigarette continued pumping smoke out.

Ernest had barely woke up. His eyes closed, and blood dried up his throat.

Meanwhile, Alter was smacked by punches over and over and over again. Thraxor then Slammed his back hard at the stairs. Followed by A Huge kick slammed on Osirus's left cheek.

Alter couldn't help but get Osirus's spine getting damaged over and over again.

The walls up the story were all Engulfed in flames.

Osirus's body was all damaged and done for.

Thraxor cocked up Osirus's spear as he walked in front. Appearing stern. His fists closed tight around the Spear handle. He swiftly slammed the spear butt, aiming up Osirus's centre of the chest.

Alter swiftly caught the spear butt close to the chest.

He pushed with all the force he could. Sending the spear of Thraxor's right fist. As Alter stood, Thraxor swiftly slammed his right Elbow up Osirus's Chest. Making him crash down the Stairs.

He then dragged Osirus up his Jacket's collar. Grabbing his right palm. As he smashed it up the flame engulfed the wooden wall.

The skin as it burned up. Grilled up. As the skin turned red and quickly brown.

Alter could feel stinging up his whole body. Alter swiftly slammed his free left palm aimed straight at Thraxor's eye. Freeing the palm.

The palm was all red and burnt. Charred abruptly, appearing like a cooked steak, medium rare.

Alter shook the Right palm. As smoke, barely visible came out.

Alter swiftly slammed Thraxor down. As he smashed his head up Thraxor's belly.

He then swiftly ran up the thrown Spear.

As he picked up the spear. He was attacked by an Assassin. As he swung a katana. As the Katana came in front of Osirus's head. Alter blocked it using the spear. Producing sparks. Alter smashed a kick up the Assassin's solar plexus. He slammed down. Sending the katana falling away.

Alter swiftly impaled the Spear butt inside the Assassin's chest. Killing him off, blood flew out as he took the spear butt out.

Sangorath came running up to Osirus, armed with a katana and he swung it up. But Alter swiftly brought the spear in between. Blocking the Katana from Osirus's throat.

Alter quickly slammed a kick up Sangorath's belly. As he moved away the spear. Sangorath swiftly disappeared, leaving red particles behind.

Back Osirus came red particles. But before Alter could react. Sangorath stabbed the katana back Osirus's hind back. The Katana blade swiftly covered up with blood. As more and more blood is drawn out.

Sangorath dragged the Katana out, leading the way to more blood dripping out.

As soon as Alter looked behind. He was slammed far as Sangorath threw a magic blow up Osirus's belly. The spear flew off his arm.

Alter swiftly stood up. Suddenly, Came red particles. From where he was slammed far. It was Bludreth who teleported up there. Then ran Atlantas who jumped straight up Osirus's head.

Slamming his elbow up Osirus's back. As he held up his hands.

Alter attempted to slam his head up and up towards Atlantas. Then finally, Alter Jumped and Slammed his parietal up Atlantas's forehead. Leaving him free. Alter Swiftly stood as he slammed a kick on Atlantas's chest. Smashing him down the wooden ground.

Alter swiftly ran as he slammed, and smashed punches and kicks over the Assassins. He ran as he went on slamming them down.

He quickly cocked the spear up and swung it in front of the Assassins. He swiftly then struck the spear blade into an Assassin up his chest.

He swiftly dragged the spear out, getting attacked by Other Assassins. He swung his spear up them. He killed an Assassin over Assassin over Assassin and Assassins.

Suddenly, he was booted with a kick up Osirus's solar plexus, crashing him down. It was Atlantas, Cocking up to a Katana. He walked out of the Assassins close to Osirus and he stared into his eyes. He stood stern as his fist cocked the katana even tighter.

He swiftly swung it up Osirus. Alter swiftly blocked Osirus's face up Using the spear. Leading the Katana striking up the spear in between. The sudden voice produced. As the sparks flew by. Alter pushed the Katana up as he stood up quickly.

He swiftly slammed a punch, crashing Atlantas far away, down the floor.

Suddenly, Bludreth ran as he swung his katana. Alter swiftly slammed the spear up between them again. Bludreth swiftly took the Katana back as he pierced it through Osirus's knee flesh. The trousers ripped, the skin cut open to a wound. Blood came out. Bending the knee a bit.

Then Bludreth swiftly began swinging the katana. Alter blocked it until finally, Bludreth slammed the Katana hard on Alter's spear. Suddenly, came a loud screeching noise. Sparks flew out. The spear broke. Two pieces formed. The spear butt and some part of the handle, one piece and the spear blade and some more part of the handle, the other piece.

Alter quickly stabbed the spear butt into Bludreth's stomach. As soon as it impaled, blood spilt out.

He then dragged the Spear butt out as he slammed Bludreth with a fierce kick, smashing him down the wooden floor.

As Alter positioned to tug on the Assassin's. Out of the crowd came an Assassin. He was cocked up to an RPG. All loaded up.

He walked closer and closer. Alter stood dead-Still.

As he approached in front. He pointed the barrel out, towards Osirus.

Alter swiftly slammed the spear blade up the handle, crashing it on the ground.

Alter swiftly crashed the Assassin down the floor, kicking him.

Another Assassin swiftly slammed a kick on Osirus. Landing on Osirus's solar plexus.

Alter swiftly turned and stabbed the spear butt handle in the Assassin's back. The handle blocked the blood Like a tourniquet.

Then, Alter violently ran. As he slammed each assassin the way. He finally reached the staircase as the Assassins ran. Suddenly the Assassin Came running, pointing the RPG up the stairs. He quickly pulled the trigger, sending a huge explosion. The orange fiery ball quickly turned red. The stairs blew. A lot of wooden pieces flew out. Alter slammed hard up to the floor from the strong explosion.

The walls of the first story broke. Wood particles fell. Assassins had fallen off. Dead or barely alive. Only for the fact that the main Assassins were alive.

Meanwhile, Alter looked behind the explosion as he relieved, breathing heavily.

He and Javon were now one staircase distant. As Alter climbed the stairs, the more they creaked.

He then swiftly ran through the whole staircase.

Meanwhile, Sangorath had reached up to Sirius's Arsenal clutching up a strong RPG. Putting the powder in it. Filling it up and it was all ready.

As soon as Alter jerked up to look around. Javon was not there. It was Shaun and Ernest tied up a log spiky from the front. Stabbed in the two's backs.

As he entered the room, he was slammed with a strong kick down the floor from the right. It was Javon, floating the Box up as he walked out, revealing himself.

He swiftly pressed down to Osirus's chest with his left leg. Pressing the cheek down harder than it already was.

Alter pushed the Leg out with all the efforts he could.

Javon grudged Osirus's shirt collar. Pulling him up.

"You made it." Said Javon "You made it in this body."

"Exactly."

Javon swiftly Slammed Osirus on Shaun.

Shaun groaned low and gasped deep as the spikes stabbed inside his whole back.

As Alter fell. Shaun stared up at him.

"You fine?" Asked Shaun barely audible "Do something towards him."

"Shut up." Said Alter.

"Go get beaten to death then."

Shaun slammed a kick up Osirus's face. Sending close to Javon. He slammed Osirus up the wall. Alter then slammed a strong punch up Javon's lips. Making him go free.

Alter stood stern As Javon stared Aggressively.

Then from the back came Red particles and revealed, that it was Sangorath as he pointed the RPG up at Osirus.

"Stop there Moron." Said Sangorath "Or else the next moment you'll be anything but alive."

"Alright." Whispered Alter.

Then Alter suddenly slammed his elbow striking at Sangorath's Intestines. Slamming him down the stairs, slipping down the stairs.

Javon swiftly Ran but was smashed with a punch up his nose.

Alter slammed Kicks over the logs the two were tied. As the logs almost got out the wooden floor.

Then Javon smashed a strong punch at Osirus's face. Blood splattered out of Osirus's nose.

Alter swiftly bent down as he clutched up to Javon's stomach. Grasping it Tightly Round.

As he attempted to push him.

Javon slammed his elbow over elbow on Osirus as he attempted to remove him. Alter had made Osirus like a zombie.

Sangorath ran in up the Stairs. He swiftly cocked the RPG as Javon Struggled. Sangorath, with no thoughts, pointed the RPG down the floor and pulled the trigger.

Sending a huge explosion. Javon and Alter flew off. Breaking through A wall. The impact removed the logs from the floor like weeds as they flew out along the two. Javon swiftly used a field to get the box back as he blew an energy blow. But Alter too used a blow. Sending them to the left-hand side of the Base. They both used their powers to break the fall. Yet failed as they still crashed down the grass, just minimal damage. Ernest and Shaun Tied up the log and were blown to the left side of the base. The floor and walls blew whole, throwing out thousands of wood pieces in the air.

In between the two's eyes was the box. The two began crawling up to the box. Javon crawled up as fast as he could. But, Alter was crawling way more swiftly as he almost reached up the box.

He swiftly put his burnt brown right-hand close the box. He quickly felt pushed over and taken over.

He was swiftly slammed over. As he flew up the sky. Looked around was red energy aura. As it flew like a rocket. It was Sangorath who swiftly dragged Osirus up the Sky along with him.

As Alter was swiftly taken away. Javon formed a wall. A red shield wall. Dividing Alter and The Assassins to the right-hand side.

The air sped behind as the two clutched up to their collars. As they flew abruptly in the air.

Suddenly Alter blew away as he separated from Sangorath. Purple dried fluid spread around. Alter quickly replenished a shield. Covering him from face to toe. As he slammed, the shield broke, he was safe. Looked at the left was the burning mansion engulfed in flames, broken and blown up in certain areas. As he looked down, he was sighted with the corpses of The Assassins from the explosion and the ones he killed off.

He found his spear handle which flew down off.

He swiftly picked it up. His burnt hand clutched it hard.

Suddenly, came red beams as The other three Assassin's landed in a horizontal row.

Atlantas, Bludreth, Thraxor and Sangorath stood stern and blood-lusted while Alter Stood alone with blood dried up his skin. He was holding up a broken spear in his burnt hand. As Alter looked stern. In an instant, the flames turned violet. As they barely glossed.

Alter stared sternly as The Assassins approached further.

Then, Alter swiftly ran, jumping over the bodies as the Assassins made a round around him.

He stopped as the four aimed the daggers at him.

Sangorath dragged his dagger up to Osirus's throat. Touching it pretty close.

As the skin pressed slightly.

Alter quickly slammed his elbow up Sangorath's belly and swung the spear behind. Slitting it through Sangorath's belly. Creating a horizontal slit, Shallow.

Alter quickly slammed a kick up Sangorath's chest, crashing him down. Alter was swiftly swung and attacked By Bludreth, who swiftly swung a dagger close to Osirus's throat. Alter swiftly slammed down the ground up his butt. Preventing the dagger from piercing into him.

He Swiftly slammed a kick up Bludreth's left calve. Resulting in him falling.

Thraxor and Atlantas swiftly swung their Daggers up fallen flat Osirus's face.

He dragged the broken spear in between. Producing sparks as they flew off and blocked the two daggers.

He swiftly pushed the two daggers up as he swiftly stood. Slamming a kick up Atlantas.

He ran up to Thraxor as he swung the Spear up him. But he quickly slammed a fierce kick up his chest. Slamming Alter Down the Ground hard on his hips.

"This Big bull." Groaned Alter slowly.

Thraxor suddenly jumped up on him. As they rolled down, he threw Alter far. He flew, slamming strong up to Javon. But a few metres close he reached Javon. Alter slammed up his back hard. A red border wall it was blocked him like a wall. Javon made it. Who was opening the box and almost there.

Alter slipped up his back down as he looked front, Thraxor came running fast. He swiftly stood as he ran extremely fast.

He swiftly Jumped up, up to Thraxor's belly, slamming hard there. They fell down to the ground, crashing down hard.

Thraxor swiftly slammed a stiff kick up his chest. Slamming him far stronger on the wall.

He swiftly stood up the wall, clutching the spear even firmer and harder, flaring his nostrils.

The burnt hand-stretched, exposing unburnt skin. All fine and fair.

He swiftly ran. So did Thraxor, they both ran as they jumped over the corpses.

Thraxor quickly threw a punch. But Alter swiftly bent his knees down, sliding through. He reached his legs. He swiftly thrust the Spear inside the left Knee. Blood drew out fast. Yet stopped like pressured water. At any time it might come out. The blood then flew down slowly like honey. Flowing down as it reached calves.

Thraxor Groaned deeply as he smashed his forehead into Osirus's, slipping his palm over the stabbed broken spear.

He stood as he dragged the spear out.

The blood flew out like medicine from the syringe.

Thraxor swiftly grabbed his throat up. Pressing it up hard.

Thraxor kept on pressing the throat as his mask emitted smoke.

Osirus's legs floated up in the air. It felt like he was being hanged up his throat with a tightrope.

Alter swung his left hand close to Thraxor's mask. Attempting to grab it out, until he realised that the mask was infused under his skin.

"You got the mask in you?" Asked Alter "I mean how the?"

"Shut it" Gasped Thraxor loud and rough.

He pressed the throat even Harder.

"Not going to change I guess." Choked Alter.

"Throw him away Thraxor!" Yelled Sangorath.

Thraxor quickly threw Alter off his clutch, slamming him down the grass.

Alter Rolled up, he jerked the spear. Pointed at Thraxor's throat.

Then, it stabbed inside. The blood came out quickly. The skin skewered with the spear. The nerves cut off from each other.

The handle had blood flowing down. Reaching Alter's hand. He pushed the spear inside harder, putting his other left hand. Thrusting the Spear even deeper. Thraxor froze dead. His body turned tinted shallow blue like poisoned. He was dead.

The Assassins were shocked. Thraxor was dead as Alter removed the spear. He crashed down to the ground. Bleeding the neck out. No life left.

Alter ran fast as the blood on the spear trailed behind.

Bludreth quickly ran in front of Osirus. Slamming up on him.

Alter quickly jerked the Spear close to Bludreth's Throat. He held it up hard as Alter applied even more force. He could barely resist. Finally, the Spear touched the throat and the voice box.

Bludreth, yet somehow held up to the Spear. Preventing it from thrusting in.

Then suddenly, a sight in the sky caught Alter's Attention. He saw a Red aura travelling up. It was Sangorath who was jumping.

As he almost reached up close. Alter swiftly swung his spear real fast. Taking the handout. As Sangorath Slammed in between.

Osirus quickly rolled up standing up.

As Sangorath looked behind at Bludreth. His throat was slit open. Blood out, dark as Molasses.

As he coughed out sounds suffocating. His Skin turning pale, he passed out. Bludreth was dead.

"Shit." Whispered Sangorath.

He quickly slammed his hand on Osirus and snatched The spear off his hands. Cocking it hard.

Alter slammed a kick up the spear. Throwing it out of His clutches.

Sangorath Swiftly cocked up Osirus's Hair. Pulling him out with him. As he walked out in the centre.

He swiftly punched up Sangorath's arm. Freeing himself out.

He stood fast up. He was quickly slammed back with a punch and smacked up his nose.

Meanwhile, Javon was pretty close to the box getting opened.

The layer of protection had become extremely thin as it appeared like thin bone-in chicken drumsticks.

He was opening the box, and behind its sight were Ernest and Shaun Tied up the log.

The rope almost burnt to ashes. As the two were free.

As He continued Opening the box, he felt everything was fine. Until the same moment. Came a blow, ocean water blue. As he lost the hold over the box. He quickly turned behind, it was Shaun. Who stood ferocious, injured and angry. He closed his fists up and furiously ran towards Javon, as he slammed a strong punch directly up his chin.

Sending Javon looking up. Yet he seemed unharmed.

"Okay, I am screwed." Sighed Shaun.

"Thanks that you realized that." Said Javon.

He swiftly slammed his elbow up Shaun's chest. Sending him crashing, metres away.

"Morons." Whispered Javon.

Shaun stood up, as he ran up to Javon again.

"Someone wants to get beaten up." Sighed Javon.

Meanwhile, Alter was fighting up to Sangorath and Atlantas. They had surrounded him from the front and back.

He slammed his right knee up Sangorath's belly as he slammed he crashed his left elbow onto Atlantas's chest.

Pushing him behind. He Slammed a strong punch At Sangorath. But no impact, he quickly crashed another fierce kick up Sangorath's belly.

As he sent him away. He quickly grabbed his collar up from behind from Atlantas, who threw his mask away.

His lips dull maroon. As he bit up to them, stern.

He quickly slammed Alter down to the ground. Smashing punches over punches unto his face, while holding his throat hard with another hand.

"Got this guy down." Gasped Atlantas.

"Great." Sighed Sangorath "Continue."

Alter swiftly pushed his knee up unto Atlantas's stomach. Finally, he slammed him out, releasing his throat. He rolled out.

Alter quickly stood up as Sangorath ran up. He stopped his punch, slamming his knee into his stomach.

Then, he took a strong pinch out of Sangorath's Belly. His muscles tightened and compacted as Alter pinched Harder over Harder.

The muscles tightened even more, as he finally Groaned. He slammed his forehead onto Osirus's forehead Hard. Leaving the pinch off. As he opened his mouth wide open. Groaning in pain.

Alter's mouth widened curved like a watermelon, smiling.

He swiftly slammed a kick into Sangorath's chest, Sending him rolling far off.

Looked behind, Atlantas walked up front. Furious and dead seriousness into his eyes.

Suddenly, the red wall appeared out, and Javon slammed Shaun onto it.

Smashing punches over punches into the solar plexus and finally sending him wrestled, rolling away.

Shaun appeared injured like dead. Close his lips, blood out. He laid down barely alive.

"Damn." Said Alter.

Atlantas caught his sight as he removed his gloves. Revealing his hands, appearing red. Seemed like blood dried of hundreds of corpses.

He closed his fists tight as he ran up to Alter. Slamming into him. Sending him into rolling rough.

He swiftly sends a fluid blow red straight at Alter's hips. Making him fall down the grass.

Sangorath came up as he slammed his leg up Osirus's head. Pressing it down hard.

"We are done Atlantas."

"Heck no." Yelled Atlantas out.

"How in the world?" Asked Sangorath confused "He's literally under my boot."

"It's not done, because I ain't killing him."

"Oh come on, don't act like an **Asshole!**"

"Just let me do the job."

"Hell no, you will screw things up."

"Sangorath!" Yelled Javon from the other side of the wall, "Just kill him and Atlantas, shut up, Don't make a mumbo jumbo out of a petty job just cause you didn't get to inagurate someone's work."

Atlantas stared dead still as he heard the statement of Javon, furious.

"The hell you staring huh?" Asked Javon "Wait! Don't do it!!"

Atlantas stared front up at Sangorath sternly.

"No! Atlantas don't, it's cocky." Yelled Sangorath "You'll mess up."

"Atlantas don't!" Screamed Javon "I won't spare you alive!"

"Atlantic Ocean!" Yelled Alter "Come here! Come on!!"

Atlantas swung a power blow unto Sangorath. So did Sangorath, he blew a huge power blow. They both collided.

Atlantas swiftly blew another power blow, sending Sangorath Off Alter's hold.

"No Atlantas Stupid!" Yelled Javon.

Sangorath rolled behind.

Alter quickly got up, removing the shoe dust pressed onto his head.

"Thanks, Atlantic Ocean for helping me out." Said Alter.

"Atlantas you son of a, I am not sparing you, You are done for!" Yelled Javon.

Atlantas Ignored him as he approached further towards Alter.

Sangorath quickly stood up, but Alter slammed a strong punch into his face, crashing him hard down the floor as blood flew out his nose.

Alter ran up to an RPG placed to his side. He cocked it up tight as he aimed it towards Atlantas, who became hostile and stood deadly. Prepared to slam Alter if he pulled the trigger.

He lowered the RPG down as he stretched his mouth muscles out and smirked.

"Slît kânthahà." He said.

As soon as Alter spoke those words, He felt a stinging and burning feeling up his throat and looked at it as a slit. Blood spiked high as it bled out fast. His body turned stiff as he gasped for breath, his life going away as his body turned pale. Crashing down to the ground, he was dead, and blood came out of his mouth.

"Ah, shit." Whispered Sangorath.

"Oh shit, This Moron, Bastard." Whispered Javon as he turned front up continuing to open the box up.

"Thank you Atlantic Ocean my guy again."

CHAPTER NINE

Sangorathbecame furious as Atlantas not only caused himself to get killed but also screwed over the Situation.

This seemed good for Alter as he was now only required to face an assassin.

Alter quickly ran as he flew up, crashing a strong kick up Sangorath's chest and holding up to the heavy Rocket Launcher.

Landing up the land, He slammed the Rocket Launcher into Sangorath. Crashing him down,

He quickly got up, booting a strong kick into Osirus's Solar plexus. throwing the Rocket Launcher out of Alter's clutches.

Alter slammed a strong kick up His chin. Spitting blood out of his mouth.

Sangorath quickly slammed his right shoulder into Osirus, Smashing him down.

He quickly stood, only to get slammed down the ground even harder with a strong smashing kick up his chest. Alter was slammed to his Solar Plexus by Sangorath with a stiff kick.

Sangorath quickly jerked his hand up to Osirus's throat. Grabbing it firm, as he pulled him up. Pushing up to his throat.

Attempting to choke him.

"You-u K-know that ain't gonna help out in that of a good way." Choked Alter.

"At least I'll finish your mannequin doing things for you as you control him." Said Sangorath "When the car's gone, what are you going to drive?"

"Absolutely Nothing!" Gasped Alter.

He swiftly pushed the right burnt Palm onto Sangorath's belly. Attempting to smack it hard.

"The hell are you doing Moron." Said Sangorath.

"Something, just something." Choked Alter.

He quickly closed the palm, slamming it onto the belly. Leaving his throat out of Sangorath's clutches. He landed up and swiftly slammed his elbow into his Solar Plexus. Followed up by Slamming his left leg by rotating around unto His Chin. Crashing him down on the grass.

Alter jumped On him. Holding him down, pressing elbows up his chest.

He quickly slammed his forehead onto his nose.

He continued slamming His Forehead onto the nose over and over.

The nose bled out, as out the nostrils, blood came down flowing, as it reached the philtrum, covered by the mask.

The blood appeared thick yet looked like Boogers.

Sangorath slammed his right knee. Just below the waist. Sending Alter out his body, rolling sideways. His back slammed hard, followed by his legs spread wide.

Sangorath jumped up, landing on his knees. Kneeling. As he stood trembling.

Alter quickly rolled backwards, standing swiftly. As Sangorath came running up, slamming a kick up his chest. Sending him pushed behind and imbalanced.

Alter quickly threw the purple energy blowout, he didn't remove it. As he kept his hand there, as it caught

Sangorath up. Quickly, the powers reduced as they sparked up. Reduced, Alter not very surprised realized what was happening.

"Oh shit." Whispered Alter "Things don't seem good."

Alter struck froze as the eyes changed up to purple, turning back to black. As he seemed to crash down to the ground. Sangorath slammed his shoulder hard onto Alter. The body fell hard. His eyes closed.

Osirus was lying down unto nothingness like a floor. He quickly woke up, because of some sensations he could feel. Looked around was pitch black. All that was a spotlight around him, Following him. He was confused as to where he was. He kept on walking in front. He felt it weird as the floor was black yet he was walking.

"The hell is this place." Said Osirus "Where is the mansion, Assassins, Shaun and Ernest?"

As he remained confused all he could remember was a strong painful hit up to his parietal and slammed into a deep pothole of water.

He quickly stopped as he sensed something strong behind him.

Then came a voice of groaning. Which caught the attention of Osirus, yet he hesitated to turn behind.

"Bro look behind." Came a deep voice.

Osirus thinking and scared finally, slowly shaking all up his body turned behind.

"Who the hell are you?" Asked Osirus as his eyes widened.

"It's me Anti-genosis No-brainer, Howdy." He said, "You can call me Alter though, even though that's why I have come here and u have woken up."

Looked at him, he was 7 feet tall. He had no skin or clothes. His whole body was coloured magenta glowing up. His eyes were white. The colour appeared with a lot of roughness as it continuously felt like thick lava.

"Oh-h s-so you are that Guy Ernest was talking about." Said Osirus anxiously.

"Um yeah but shut up, I don't have time to introduce myself and now listen without uttering some doubts." Said Alter.

"What's the deal?" Asked Osirus.

"Basically, you were knocked out by the Assassins." Said Alter.

"I was What?" Asked Osirus "By Assassins?"

"Shut up, just listen to the point." Said Alter "I have saved you from dying and currently you are fighting one Assassin and since I am fighting with your body, something is going wrong."

"Like what?"

"I can't explain now, but long story short I want you to come back to consciousness cause, If I continue being in your body, eventually I am gonna drain out and the powers will be over." Said Alter, "All you got to do is just fight that guy."

"Hell no."

"Why, 'cause you have that bloody anxiety?" Said Alter.

"You don't know 7-foot tall troll."

"Come back again bro, I know every single thing about you more than your mom and dad ever did cause well.. they are dead."

"come again?"

"Oh nothing, but what I want to tell is that-"

"I ain't coming!" Said Osirus loudly.

"Why cause you scared of fighting him." Said Alter "he's unarmed Coward!"

"Doesn't matter, They are Assassins." Shouted Osirus "Assassins, they have their trump cards in their hoods, in fact, they are trump cards by themselves."

"Exactly." Said Alter,

"Wait? What the hell do you mean?"

"They are **Ass-Ass**-ins."

"Oh come on 7-foot tall tree, do you even have something in your head, making stupid jokes." Said Osirus frustrated "I ain't coming."

"You will regret your choice." Said Alter.

"Why?"

"Cause I am anyways going to wear off at some point and going to lose control over you and would take me a while to come back"

"Why?" Asked Osirus

"Because coward, I am not your Alter Ego." Said Alter "I was never meant to."

"Then why do you tell me to call you alter huh?"

"Cause it sounds good, doesn't it?"

"Then what's your purpose huh?" Asked Osirus "Dancing while I endure the pain?"

"Dawg, we are meant to provide our users with powers." Said Alter "Even though we can take over your bodies, it's for emergency purposes and you allow that thing."

"I don't care, go back and fight the guy yourself." Said Osirus.

"No, I don't recommend it Osirus I will give you powers but-"

Osirus crashed a strong punch into Alter's stomach, making a shockwave.

"Shut up, do what I say!" Yelled Osirus out.

"Fine." Sighed Alter, "Doing as you wish."

Suddenly the place began shaking.

"Why the hell is this place shaking?" Asked Osirus.

"I guess that Sangorath is doing chest compressions."

"Wait what." Said Osirus "He considers me on his side."

"Of course not fool." Said Alter, "He must be breaking your ribs."

"What the hell, Go and stop him then Bloody fool!" Yelled Osirus.

"Oh yeah sorry."

Alter quickly reduced into Magenta particles. He was gone.

"Weird Troll." Said Osirus "Bloody Shit."

Sangorath was punching Osirus's chest.

Suddenly, Osirus's eyes opened wide up as Alter took the control back.

He swiftly slammed his forehead onto Sangorath's. crashing him out of his Body.

He quickly Stood up and stretched his hands out.

"Well, Ribs aren't broken." Said Alter.

Sangorath stood up and slammed up a Strong kick, straight unto Osirus's Schlong, Sending Alter kneeling.

"Crap." Groaned Alter "Osirus is done for."

He quickly stood up, Smashing a strong kick up Sangorath's chest.

Alter looked up to his left, the mansion's walls and roofs were all burnt. All that was left were the pillar-like structures on all the sides.

The fires had eaten up the whole mansion, Engulfing it whole.

He was quickly slammed down the ground with a push-up by Sangorath.

He was shook by the slam. He swiftly kicked Sangorath down to the grass.

Alter Turned behind. Looking behind, he was shaken by the fact that Javon was almost there as the grills were barely visible. With the red glowing ball visible even more, Glowing bright.

He quickly ran up. Slamming his shoulders like a battering ram. This made the boundary shield visible which seemed like a difficult job as it didn't break even after ramming the shoulder thrice.

Javon didn't seem to be interrupted by the fact of a 26-year-old Ramming up to his shield. As he opened the layers over layers.

Alter was quickly slammed with a strong kick by Sangorath unto his butt. Pushing him hard the shield. His right cheek stretched out.

He came out and swung a strong kick over, but it was dodged by Him. Sangorath Slammed a strong kick into his chest.

Alter quickly seemed to be kneeling. As he was feeling weak.

Alter was slammed with another Punch from his chin.

Then Sangorath quickly grabbed Alter's throat, pressing it hard and grabbing him up.

Alter then suddenly looked behind Sangorath. Blurred, he saw Assassins armed up. Coming up to him. Cocked with A24 rifles.

Seeing this, he quickly slammed his forehead into Sangorath's. Loosening the grip unto his neck. He quickly slammed his leg onto Sangorath's solar plexus followed by ramming him down with shoulders.

As Sangorath collapsed hard on the ground. Alter rolled up to the RPG. He pointed it at the Horizontally aligned Assassins armed as they aimed their guns.

Alter quickly pulled the trigger. The fireball with purple flames slammed into one of the Assassins. The ball blew up huge, amplified even more with Alter's powers, blowing all the Armed Assassins dead. Either blown up, engulfed in flames or dead on impact.

The flames quickly evaporated, revealing the dead Assassins fallen to the ground.

The explosion instantly killed all the Assassins.

Alter turned behind, walking close to Sangorath. Who struggled to wake up. Alter sprinted, Slamming a kick into his face, Breaking the mask off.

Saliva spat out his mouth. Followed up with blood flowing out his dried lips dehydrated like a famine, it was a deep cut.

Alter then pressed his leg up to his parietal. As the leg pressed down. The more Sangorath clinched up his life.

Suddenly, bullets flew, hitting the ground around. The dirt flew up, rubble blowing around. Alter quickly incepted a shield. Blocking the bullets.

Sighted around, came an Assassin. Topped with a Black robe, wearing a black mask, Pointing up An A24 Rifle. It was Sirius, who constantly fired.

As he walked, his legs smashed into a small water pond. Splashing the water up, his red glowing eyes stared straight At Osirus.

Alter quickly ran up, close to Sirius. He jumped up to the side In the air, he quickly pulled the trigger, pulling out bullets. But Alter jerked the Shield up the Side. Blocking the bullets. Alter quickly ran up and he smashed the Shield up to Sirius, Breaking it into particles as it disappeared. He quickly cocked the A24 hard, as he held the barrel up the air. He slammed a strong punch into Sirius's face. He caught hold of the pointed part of the mask as he pulled him up to his forehead, slamming it hard. He pulled the mask out as he threw it, revealing Sirius's lips, surrounded by the black beard.

Alter, with all the force he could pull the A24 out, successfully snatched it out of his hands.

He quickly aimed it at Upto Sirius, who quickly teleported as the trigger was pressed. Firing Bullets quickly. The Magazine got empty, the bullets all over. Sirius quickly came behind Alter, pressing his throat hard with his shoulders. Alter slammed his Butt behind, Slamming up to Sirius's Schlong.

He quickly pushed the shoulders out of his neck's clutch. As he turned behind, Slamming a strong kick unto Sirius's Solar plexus, throwing him 3 metres away.

Alter quickly rammed up to the Shield boundary. Cracking it up. He used a heavy amount of energy, moving like smoke.

Sangorath and Sirius quickly ran towards Alter. They quickly caught hold of Both his hands. Alter still held up as he crashed his legs over the shield. Now the shield had become extremely fragile. He pushed both the Assassins away. As he rammed strongly into the boundary. Sirius and Sangorath quickly jumped up his legs, holding up his sneakers. The Boundary, as it cracked and destroyed. Alter attempted to touch Javon. But he was thrown away on the right side. Crashing up his back hard.

Sirius crashed up towards the left side while Sangorath was beside Alter.

Alter swiftly jerked his palm up. But to no avail,

Powers didn't come out. Slowly the vision blurred as Alter passed out. Leaving the body Unconscious.

"Yes!" Yelled Sangorath as he stood up clutching to his left knee "We did it!"

"This guy." Sighed Sirius "Made me gasp, but he was destined to lose."

"Good Job." Said Javon who continued Opening the box.

"So..." Said Sangorath and Sirius.

"What the hell is So about?" Asked Javon.

"You giving us the part of the powers in that box for what we fought."

Javon stopped opening the box up as he looked at both the Assassins.

Meanwhile, Shaun was badly injured and stood up to his knees while still struggling to stand up as he felt extreme cramps in his whole body. Ernest had woken up though as he pointed his finger up to Javon.

"Say Something." Said Sangorath.

"Yeah, the part." Said Javon "The part, The part, You'll get it."

"Thanks." Panted Sirius.

"Yes." gasped Sangorath.

"In your dreams Scums." Said Javon "Rot in Hell Morons."

Javon quickly dragged a Glock out. Shooting it through Sangorath's skull. Instantly killing him. The bullet pierced through his forehead's centre. He quickly collapsed. He quickly jerked to the left as he fired two bullets into Sirius's Skull. Killing him off. He threw the Glock behind furiously.

"Bastards." Whispered Javon as he continued Opening the box.

Shaun slowly rose as he stared focused and dead-still into Javon.

"I know you are going to Slam me, Just try."

"Exactly." Giggled Shaun "I got you Prick."

"Shaun!" Yelled Ernest.

He quickly ran up to the box. He jumped up to the box, snatching it away. Shaun quickly threw a power blow to Javon, sending him down the ground. As Ernest landed, he quickly pressed his hands onto the top of the box and his eyes turned ice blue.

"Villúptâm!" Shouted Ernest.

Suddenly, the Box gave out a white flash, as it disappeared into particles in the thin air. Suddenly, Blood came out of Ernest's abdomen. Spreading to the throat. It quickly dried off as Ernest crashed onto his face to the grass.

The box was destroyed.

"Yes." Sighed Shaun.

"Yeah Absolutely yeah." Said Javon "Now this rascal hell yeah."

Javon quickly dragged up Osirus and he knocked him far. He created a strong boundary, leaving the two behind them. Shaun swiftly ran as he slammed punched over punches, attempting to break the shield open. Ernest as he looked around and realized, rammed strong up to the shield.

As the two rammed the boundary over and over again. Osirus woke up.

"What the hell." Whispered Osirus "What is happening, Argh it hurts everywhere."

"Listen You Osirus, I guess that's what's your name." Said Javon "You are done for, scoundrel."

Osirus looked behind as Ernest and Shaun panicked up to open the Shield.

"Stop, Shut there guys!" Shouted Osirus.

Osirus as he made his mind up walked in front of Javon, who was all furious and gone crazy.

He ran up to Javon as he jumped up with the kick, who quickly jerked off the place.

Javon quickly slammed his right Elbow. Throwing Osirus onto his knees hard. As he removed his hood.

He quickly dragged Osirus up his collar. As he slammed his elbow onto his nape even harder. He almost tripped.

Javon slammed a punch into his Solar plexus. Sending him groaning, clutching up his stomach as he appeared in extreme agony.

Ernest and Shaun stared in pain as their friend was being beaten up his ass.

"Osirus!" Yelled Shaun "Slam a kick into down there."

"Osirus!" Screamed Ernest.

Osirus was being slammed with punches over punches into his nose.

Blood flew out his nose as his vision became a bit blurry.

Javon slammed a kick into his chest. Crashing him down the grass.

Osirus still endured the pain as he stood up struggling to stay stable yet enduring the agony.

"You are a freak Javon! If that's your name you are a damn freak!" Yelled Osirus "You can't do shit to me, come here!"

Javon quickly landed a strong punch on his chin. Making him split blood out. Suddenly, came a strong cracking voice. Osirus could instantly feel his mouth hurting. His cheeks paining more than ever. Blood came out of his mouth. His Gum broke out.

"Come back." Said Javon "Come Back again!"

Osirus still ran up to Javon, finally crashing a strong punch on his chin.

He quickly slammed his chest onto his chest. Slamming him down to the ground.

Javon went down as he turned Osirus's face facing up the grass Javon crashed his face onto the floor. He walked around smiling at Shaun and Ernest. They had lost hope as they regretted not saving Osirus.

Osirus pressed his hands to the grass as he attempted to wake up. Javon quickly jumped onto him. Crashing him hard to the ground.

As he stretched his legs and arms out, feeling calm.

Osirus's hands soon released purple fluids as he stood up. Javon quickly jumped up. Slamming another punch. Sending Osirus Into Unconsciousness. He threw him like nothing to the wall. Smashing him hard to the grass.

Javon got his Glock. Cocked it. As he aimed it towards Osirus. He dragged a cigarette out. Putting it in between the lips. The Cigarette lit red as smoke came out quickly.

He quickly pulled the trigger shooting into his chest.

The four consecutive bullets pierced, and stuck into Osirus's chest. Making him look dead.

"Osirus!" Yelled Ernest.

"No!" Screamed Shaun "Osirus!!!"

Javon pumped the smoke as he smiled. The smoke pumped in higher proportions.

The two broke down, closing their eyes and panting quickly.

Suddenly, the bullets popped out. Even before Blood could skewer, it froze and patched. Osirus's Eyes opened as magenta fluid moved around. He began coming up. Without using anything.

Javon was shaken seeing it, he quickly shot 2 bullets. But they deflected off.

The shield boundary broke off.

Shaun and Ernest were shocked too.

Alter had returned.

He quickly slammed a punch into Javon's face. Throwing the Cigarette out of his mouth. He quickly landed a strong kick up to his Solar plexus. Slamming him on the ground.

Javon swiftly stood, slamming a strong kick unto him, crashing him on the grass on his butt.

Shaun and Ernest quickly came throwing power blows on Javon. Keeping him back.

"Listen here, You two." Muttered Alter "We have to kill him together. First, make him unarmed."

Shaun quickly threw another blow, throwing the gun off Javon's hand.

"Let's do it and finish him for once and all."

"Now that's what Osirus lacks." Said, Shaun.

"Come back?"

"Nothing." Said, Shaun.

"Stand fast Bro." Said Ernest.

The three stood together.

As Javon stood. The three quickly ran up to him. Slamming punches. Kicking him. Alter pushed him, ramming him with his shoulders.

Ernest quickly slammed a kick on Javon's solar plexus.

He quickly threw out a strong power blow unto the three, pushing them behind.

Alter contemplated for a second. Until he quickly dragged Shaun's collar.

"Hey, What you doing?" Asked Shaun

"Giving you something back."

"What?"

"Throwing you."

Alter quickly threw Shaun like a guitar on Javon. Slamming him hard on the ground.

Alter quickly ran up to Javon. Dragging him up. Slamming his forehead. He slammed Javon even farther with a push. As he continued pushing him. They reached the edge of the cliff. Alter brought him down to his knees. All his face was covered with bruises. His mouth turned purple.

"Bring the Damn gun." Muttered Alter.

Ernest ran up as he came with the Glock.

"You are done for." Muttered Alter.

He caught the Glock. Cocking it. He pushed it down into Javon's mouth. The barrel was all warm enough to flash out the bullets. Alter quickly pulled the trigger. And boom! Bullets over bullets fired. Until one bullet was left. With 5 bullets fired into the mouth. Javon was all dead.

His body floated like a hanged corpse.

Alter as he walked behind. Looked up towards Javon. His mouth pumping out smoke.

He quickly slammed a strong kick. Sending him to even more the edge. He fired the final bullet. And Javon was out the cliff, falling off and disappearing into the trees. Alter threw the Glock off the cliff.

"Finally I am done." Sighed Alter.

He was gone as Osirus came back to Consciousness.

As he woke up, he was Scared to be close to the cliff.

"Holy shit, What the F-" Muttered Osirus before crashing behind to Unconsciousness.

The Mansion had burnt whole. As the sun rose, Giving light. With the Assassins dead.

Epilogue

3 days had passed since the trio attacked the Assassins. Inside the tent. Shaun and Ernest sat up eating rice.

In front of them, was Osirus laying straight.

He woke up and looked into his body. He was donned with a Blue t-shirt and pants. His right hand was all covered with bandages.

"Where the hell are we?" Asked Osirus "Argh! My jaw!"

Ernest choked as he heard Osirus. Shaun kept his rice cup away as they both came walking towards Osirus.

"Finally, You're fine."

"Why the hell am I on a mattress."

"Well... What do you remember?" Questioned Ernest.

"Getting some crazy pain in my parietal." Said Osirus "Why?"

"Exactly." Said, Shaun.

"But why everything except that part is hurting huh?"

"Well, you have some injuries like deep cuts, stabs, 2nd-degree burn in your palm and another thing." Said, Shaun.

"Oh so that's why it's wrapped up, but why do I have all this shit?"

"Cause you fought, I mean Anti-Genosis fought."

"Oh, so he met me." Said Osirus "Wait, he did what??!"

"Fought." Said Ernest.

"Holy shit." Said Osirus "But why my body, it's me who's getting screwed over."

"Bro shut up with your anxiety, it's annoying." Said, Shaun.

"Got a point though." Said Osirus "Because No civil guy saw it, but why the hell is my Jaw Hurting like anything."

"Well, we'll talk later." Said, Shaun.

"No you ain't going anywhere or I'll tell Alter to chase ya."

"Fine." Sighed Shaun.

"Your Gum came out." Said Ernest.

"My what came out!" Snapped Osirus.

"Gum." Said, Shaun.

"Oh no!" Panicked Osirus "My Gum!"

"It ain't a big deal." Said Ernest "You have a new gum."

"But it's not real though." Said Osirus "And I am not even 70 years old to lose teeth."

"Just accept the fate bro, We didn't cause it." Said, Shaun.

"Fine." Sighed Osirus "So when are we going to reach the Wizard Slash Sorcerer?"

"Tomorrow." Said Ernest "Because you have Almost Recovered."

"Oh yeah, it feels good." Said Osirus "Now let me rest."

"Fine, no issues we'll eat our rice." Said Ernest.

Osirus rested while the other two devoured the smooth soft rice.

❧❧❧

Meanwhile, at the base, the Assassins corpses were all laid down. The Mansion was reduced to Ashes.

All of a sudden came Assassins walking. And in the centre, was An Assassin. His hair was grey from the sides. He had cocked up to a Katana. As he stood at the Cliff's edge.

"Scorpious's guys have done this." Said the Assassin "But they are not gonna stay alive."

Then came an Assassin out of the crowd as he said "How the hell we gonna track them down."

"We will find them. Cuz they can't do shit, they will eventually run into... **Us.**"

He turned his head behind. His beard around his lips. His eyes appeared green as he was looking deadly.....

OSIRUS
PART TWO

Afterword

This book is been in working for 2 damn whole years. No seriously, I mean the book's writing didn't take 2 years, that thing just took a few months. The thing was that first, this book was meant to be a Manga. But only for me to realize my crap drawing skills plus for a series like Osirus, it won't be great for me. So I decided to write it and anyways, I have been obsessed with storytelling since I was a small kid. I have read story books before so for me writing a book wouldn't be hard. It was just the fact that I had to learn it. So I watched Tutorials from Writers like Brandon McNulty, Jenna Moreci and some more. These videos helped me improve my Book's content and execution. To be honest It wasn't just the manga writing that took me 2 years. Another thing that delayed this book was me *"Yapping"* about this. I messaged Shamit constantly about the plot characters etc and he was always annoyed by the fact that I yap a lot, he went like "Bro stop with the yapping and Write!" Until one day I got motivated to sit on my butt and write and so I wrote the first page, Aka the prologue and It was bad. Shamit rewrote it to make it sound better. He even rewrote the first page of chapter 1. He always gave me feedback and annoyed by the fact that when is the Book was getting Published and now he may be reading it and his soul attained to peace after 2 years. In short It's been a Great, Agonizing & all at once Journey writing this book.

Hope you enjoyed it :)

Your Regards,

Bodh Chandramani Sonavane.

About The Author

Bodh Sonavane is a 13-year-old teenager. Who writes in the fiction genre.
Currently, he lives with his parents in Maharashtra, India.